1st 1986

£5

PARLOUR 4
and other stories

BY THE SAME AUTHOR:

Novels

MARK LAMBERT'S SUPPER
THE GUARDIANS
A USE OF RICHES
THE MAN WHO WON THE POOLS
THE LAST TRESILIANS
AN ACRE OF GRASS
THE AYLWINS
VANDERLYN'S KINGDOM
AVERY'S MISSION
A PALACE OF ART
MUNGO'S DREAM
THE GAUDY
YOUNG PATTULLO
A MEMORIAL SERVICE
THE MADONNA OF THE ASTROLABE
FULL TERM
ANDREW AND TOBIAS
A VILLA IN FRANCE
AN OPEN PRISON
THE NAYLORS

Short Stories

THE MAN WHO WROTE DETECTIVE STORIES
CUCUMBER SANDWICHES
OUR ENGLAND IS A GARDEN
THE BRIDGE AT ARTA
MY AUNT CHRISTINA

PARLOUR 4

and other stories

by

J. I. M. STEWART

LONDON

VICTOR GOLLANCZ LTD

1986

First published in Great Britain in 1986
by Victor Gollancz Ltd,
14 Henrietta Street, London WC2E 8QJ

British Library Cataloguing in Publication Data
Stewart, J. I. M.
Parlour 4 and other stories
I. Title
823'.912[F] PR6037.T466

ISBN 0-575-03735-0

Photoset and printed in Great Britain by
Photobooks (Bristol) Ltd

CONTENTS

PARLOUR 4

AT THE HYDRO we commonly had Parlour 4. There were several of these larger, and presumably more expensive, bedrooms on the ground floor—the idea no doubt being that their occupants thus had access to most of the public rooms (lounges, dining-room, ball-room, billiard-room and so on) as well as to the gardens and woodland walks surrounding the place, without having to put up with the fatigue of staircases. With my father it was chiefly, I suspect, a matter of prestige. Parlour 4 was the largest of these superior rooms, and he was displeased if it had been booked by somebody else. My father was, among other things, a local lad who made good. He was fond of calling himself a 'Moray loon'.

But there was one point of economy about the arrangement. A Parlour was large enough to harbour, as well as a married couple, a child or even a couple of children. This was quite a common disposition of things in Scotland in those days. I was an only child, with a bed in Parlour 4 as a matter of course: this still when I was a boy of six or even seven, and was perhaps beginning to think the arrangement a demeaning one. I am fairly sure that I graduated to a room of my own in the hydro on the holiday immediately following the one with which I am concerned here.

The hydros were rather different from the hotels, and I liked them better: particularly the one in Moray. The hotels to which we frequently went were at seaside places, and if I had no aversion to the North Sea in itself—and particularly to a pottering sort of fishing from a rowing-boat—I did hate my obligatory immersions in those icy waters. Nor did I make much of the crowds of bucket-and-spade children on the beaches, being rather shy and tardy with miscellaneous acquaintances in general. The surroundings of the hydro were quite different: pine woods with many winding paths in them along which I could wander in solitude but seldom without reassuring glimpses through the trees of the big white building itself. At home in Edinburgh I used to lie in bed longing for our next visit to these with an intensity, a passion, which returns to me quite vividly now, some sixty years later. Like Wordsworth in his poem, I cannot paint what then I was, in this feeling for the sights and scents and rustlings of external nature. But with this, although I pause to mention it, there is little connection with what I am going to record.

The hydro itself had more commonplace attractions. The public rooms seemed to me enormous but at the same time friendly. There were the mysterious 'baths', full of odd devices and smelling of mountains of hot towels, to which my father would companion me every morning. The dining-room had a large flat roof to which there was access up an external spiral staircase, and from one point I could glimpse on a nearby hill a curious tower known as the Nelson Monument. When I discovered that I could make my way to this, that its door (flanked by two small cannon) stood open, and that by climbing to its battlements I could look straight at what I thought of as the North Pole, my happiness in my solitude was entire.

In a seaside hotel it seemed to be the convention that each couple or family largely kept itself to itself, with little more than civil exchanges on one's way in or out of a dining-room. In a hydro (perhaps as a matter of tradition percolating from the 'watering places' of England) there was much more of sociable getting together. This was true of tennis courts and croquet lawns and bowling greens and billiard tables—at all of which people picked up partners in a companionable way. Children of my own age made their first indulged essays on these. In my earliest teens I was to become quite an accomplished billiard-player, although I have seldom had a cue in my hands since.

Our days, of course, were not spent exclusively on these diversions. Both my parents had a good many relations within visiting distance, and in the course of three weeks or a month we would call on most of them in some style. 'Style' meant a hired carriage-and-pair—the two horses being excused by the mildly hilly character of the region. I recall very little of the people with whom we thus went to lunch or tea, but I do now realize that they were a surprisingly mixed crowd. Some lived in large houses and owned numerous dogs. Others were much less assuming; their parlours and kitchens and farmyards harboured a variety of smells which equally stimulated my curiosity and offended my taste. And one individual I do remember very well: a middle-aged man who had contrived in youth to spike his wrist with a dirty pitch-fork (a difficult feat when one attempts to visualize it) and who thus exhibited a hideous deformity whenever he passed the butter, or pressed upon me a bowl of geans—a species of wild cherry agreeable in itself but surprisingly apt to make a small boy rapidly feel rather sick.

I now know that the grander people were connected with my mother and the humbler with my father. But he, at least, gave very little sign of being affected at all by this unusual breadth to our social spectrum. He was a sculptor by profession, and already of considerable eminence. He liked, I imagine, to exhibit the classlessness of what used to be called Bohemia. This—perhaps oddly—inclined him at times to doggedly extravagant behaviour: for example, spouting in public more or less topical passages from *Macbeth*, or kissing a serving wench behind a scullery screen, or even shocking our fellow-guests by some ingenious breach of their proprieties. He was also fond of what he called sometimes a 'dram' and sometimes a 'peg'. He judged this dash of whisky—as did most of our hosts—to be an appropriate stirrup cup on departure.

On both the outward and the inward legs of these expeditions I was commonly allowed to sit on the box beside the driver—a position from which it was no doubt possible to obtain an extensive view of the surrounding countryside. What more commanded my attention, however, was the behaviour of the two mares, the hindquarters of which were jogging along in front of me. I admired the grace with which now one and now the other elevated its tail, disclosed peculiarities of anatomy unsuspected to a normal view, and effortlessly defecated (but never staled) without altering its pace in any way. I mention this trivial and even disagreeable circumstance in compensation for what, later on, some readers may regard an an inadequate interest in certain conceivably sexual undertones of my narratives.

On these drives my grandmother, for some reason, seldom accompanied us. And now I find that I have, through sheer inexpertness, failed so much as to mention the old lady! She was my grandmother on the maternal side; she lived for the greater part of the year totally inert in a small house in Elgin, ministered to by two maids; and when we were at the hydro she would frequently join us for a week's 'rest' there. She was a simple-minded old soul, and presently I shall have to touch her in when mentioning a small episode which reflects, I fear, very adversely on my juvenile character. I have already exhibited myself—have I not?—in a glancing way as a somewhat shy and sensitive child. It is with regret that I shall reveal that I was rather a sly child as well.

And now I return to the main scene of my story.

The hydro employed a lady who was called, I think, the Entertainer. She did herself occasionally entertain to the extent of giving short 'recitals' on the piano, but her chief task was to devise and promote entertainments engaged in by the guests themselves. As most of these were normally staid Scots, and as the Scottish ethos is commonly and justly thought of as on the dour side, her employment might readily be imagined as a not particularly grateful one. But this wasn't so. Miss McPhail was much admired for having no end of 'go', and she could regularly coax the great majority of us into a surprising variety of evening gaieties. The chief of these was dancing, and for this almost nightly diversion the hydro ran to a small orchestra. Although without much experience of social behaviour, I believe I was often surprised by the *brio* which quite elderly people normally of the quietest comportment put into waltzing and the new-fangled fox-trot, and even more into what some enthusiastic Gaelic bard has called 'hurricanes of Highland reels'. I didn't myself much like the dances with a single partner, since I found stumbling gyratings with a small girl embarrassing rather than pleasurable. Indeed, if I remember aright, the mere taking of the floor for such a purpose often had the odd effect of making me positively fail to hear the music: a decided disability in a dancing man. But I was all right at the foursomes and eightsomes, and could even join my high treble to the hoots and yells prescriptive from the male participants. There was a quieter form of Scottish country-dance called the 'Haymakers' which I particularly enjoyed.

For those guests—elderly for the most part—who cared neither to dance nor watch dancing there was a 'card room' which I was told I must by no means enter, and which rather suggested to my mind a chapel set aside for private prayer and devotion, although those frequenting it no doubt did so in the interest of whist, bridge, or some popular card game of the moment. But there was a further and much larger room known as the 'badminton room', in which shuttlecocks could be banged to and fro across a net on days too wet or windy for this exercise out of doors. It was the place of principal resort on nights upon which there was no dancing, and it was here that Miss McPhail chiefly came into her own, organizing all sorts of paper games for young and old alike. But she was far from stopping at that. We were divided into sides for playing dumb crambo or enacting charades, and a few guests even improvised little sketches dignified with the title of 'private theatricals'. These latter were disapproved of by others, on principles suggesting that our Scottish post-Edwardian world remained not all that far from *Mansfield Park*. This much amused my father, whose own standards, I suppose, were those of his fellow-artists in Edinburgh. Incidentally, it was my noticing how he had to be careful at not too quickly guessing words and finding rhymes and so on in the paper games that first instructed me that he was a man whose abilities didn't stop short at the use of mallet and chisel. So far as I can remember, he even avoided ever emerging as the winner of a game called 'Guess Who I Am'.

'Guess Who I Am' was not a complicated game, and its title is almost self-explanatory. Miss McPhail possessed a large number of sheets of paper, on each of which was written the name of some more or less celebrated person, whether male or female, living or dead. One of these papers she would pin to the back of everybody taking part, and everybody would then hurry round asking everybody else questions like 'Am I British?' or 'Am I a famous highwayman?' or the like, which had to be truthfully answered by the person interrogated. As soon as one believed that one had thus arrived at one's identity one hurried off to Miss McPhail, who credited one with a mark if one was right, and substituted a new name for the detected one.

In this game, which was a very light-hearted affair, I was allowed to join, although my knowledge of celebrities was inevitably extremely limited. Quite soon, however, I suddenly began to score, and it is here that my confession of precocious moral turpitude must be made.

My grandmother on her visits to the hydro took no active part in any of these diversions, and had indeed a very imperfect notion of what was going on. She did, however, like to sit by the wall and watch. She liked watching 'Guess Who I Am', and there came an occasion upon which an impulse of quite innocent affection prompted me to attempt drawing her into it as she sat. So I went up to her, turned my back, and was about to devise some appropriate question when she herself spoke on a note of gentle surprise.

'Dear me!' my grandmother said, 'Lord Roberts of Kandahar! Now, fancy that.'

I realized in a flash that the old lady had no notion of the game, but that the appearance of her grandson with a little label on his back came to her as something like a simple exercise in reading. So I kissed my grandmother (I blush as I record the fact now) and hurried off to Miss McPhail.

'I'm Lord Roberts,' I said—and with hideous cunning gave the impression that 'Kandahar' was beyond me. I got my mark at once. Miss McPhail clearly felt that here was a clever little boy. With a new name on my back, I asked appropriate childish questions of several players before once more presenting myself to my grandmother.

'Well, I declare,' my grandmother said. 'Mr George Meredith!'

Inevitably, I quickly overreached myself. (I think it was when I told Miss McPhail that I was Lilly Langtry.) The Entertainer tumbled to what was going on, and gently told me to remove myself from the game. Unfortunately, my mother by some means became aware of my iniquity at once, and there and then packed me off to bed in disgrace. My father wouldn't have been pleased by my exploit, but he would have laughed it off, and let be—in which case my mother, whom I knew to be far from the dominant one of the pair, would have acquiesced without fuss. So the way it actually fell out was what schoolboys at that time would have called hard cheese. I was upset, and sulked for days. And upon this, there was a further penalty. It was decided that the mischief had resulted from my being 'over-excited', and that an earlier bed-time must be the rule for the rest of the holiday. So instead of being allowed up till nine or later I had to be in bed in Parlour 4 by half-past eight. All this made me believe—of course quite mistakenly—that the entire hydro was aware of my absurd cheating and was laughing at me. Abruptly, my small paradise had turned into something quite different.

And needless to say, I had no further truck with the Entertainer's entertainments. The mere half-hour after dinner now allowed me before retiring to Parlour 4 I spent in a room actually labelled 'Reading Room', struggling through *Black Beauty*, which seemed to be the autobiography of a horse, and which I had lately been given as a prize at the end of my first year at a kind of baby-school. It was a dull occupation after having so lately been Lord Roberts of Kandahar. Had child psychologists existed in those days they might possibly have described me as 'disturbed'. Certainly my sleeping-habits were upset. Usually I was sound asleep in my alcove in Parlour 4 long before my parents came to bed. Now, I was sometimes still awake. And sometimes, too, I woke up in the darkness of midnight, and didn't like that at all.

' . . . *softening of the brain* . . . '

The words came to me out of near-darkness in Parlour 4. I suppose that some low bedside lamp had been left on, and that my parents were preparing to get into the big bed at the other end of the room. I suppose that I had come awake just before the words were spoken. It was my mother who had spoken them in what she must have thought (if she thought at all) was a voice much too low to rouse me.

'I tell you, Jamie, softening of the brain. If you don't stop now, within five years the whisky will have killed you.'

The chill horror that instantly overwhelmed me on hearing these words, I have to trust my reader to achieve some sense of. It was a sudden apocalypse of dereliction and dismay, an instant crumbling of the entire world I knew. But what followed was—if it be conceivable—more terrifying, more annihilating of the very roots of my being, still. My father spoke in penitence, pledging himself to reform. But he did this in a tone utterly alien to my whole conception of him: a whining, cringing, subservient tone. My own heart seemed to shrink within me as I heard it.

And it went on. My mother began again about *softening of the brain*; my father whined and blubbered. My sense of time dissolved into a meaningless eternity of anguish. And then—I suppose—I fell asleep.

When I woke up next morning it was at the normal time, but to an instant memory of an experience which I knew must transform my entire life. I was the son, the only child, of a man likely to die a drunkard's death. I had seen drunkards in the streets of Edinburgh on several occasions—chiefly when being driven home from a party in a cab which had necessarily to traverse some mean streets on the journey. Something nasty, I now knew, must already have been happening to their brains—and was due to happen to my father's brain if he didn't change his ways. It was a stiff piece of knowledge to have come suddenly to a small boy in the night. A skilled writer could probably wring a good deal of pathos out of it. But now, looking back on those hours, those days, from the threshold of old age, I seek for some sort of precision in the experience, and grope after distinctions. Overwhelming as was the relevation of my father's peril, it was less utterly crushing than the memory of his mere manner during the episode. He was by nature a commanding, although by no means arrogant, man. He ruled us—my mother and myself—with an easy good humour which we would never have dreamed of challenging. He had his quirks and oddities, and we loved him for them. Now, there had been this: the weak and maudlin self-reproaches, the whining, the patently hopeless promises of reform. Suddenly, and as if revealed by a flash of lightning, was somebody closer to me than a brother or sister would have been—and somebody I had never known.

Before breakfast, he and I went as usual to the baths. His manner was wholly normal, so that I found myself covertly scanning his figure, his face, for small indications that might hint the truth. I noticed for the first time certain minute and zigzag red lines on his nose. They could even be distinguished—but only just—on cheeks wholesomely bronzed from our holiday in the sun. And he certainly didn't dodder or totter, or stutter in the uttering of his customary idle and cheerful remarks. It hadn't come to that. Not yet. There was an old man whose duty it was officiously to wrap our naked bodies in unnecessarily voluminous bath-robes before conducting us from one chamber to another. (The place, after all, was a hydropathic, and there were rituals to observe.) I wondered whether the old man also was destined to go soft in the brain.

At breakfast, my mother, too, seemed her usual composed self. This added to my horror. If in an unformulated way, I must have wondered how any faithful and affectionate wife could live on undisturbed—or with even the public appearance of being undisturbed—having the ghastly knowledge she had. I ate my porridge, with its allotted teaspoonful of brown sugar and tot of cream, almost unaware of what I did: said I wasn't hungry for finnan-haddie; escaped from table as quickly as I could. I went outside, and presently found myself on that flat roof to the dining-room: a spot where I felt tolerably secure of solitude, since I seemed to be the only person to whom it ever occurred to mount the spiral staircase giving access to it. I paced the roof from side to side, mechanically re-enacting a small fantasy I had invented not long before. I was an admiral pacing his quarter deck, pausing now to gaze out to port and now to starboard, eager to descry an enemy sail. It was of course the Nelson Monument that had bred this small piece of theatre. And there, now, its battlements just visible above the fir trees, the Monument was. Had it not been in view, my mind might never have evolved the notions it now did.

Nelson had been a hero. That was why the people of a nearby little town had built the thing. Probably Lord Roberts of Kandahar had been a hero too. Could I possibly, in the appalling situation in which I found myself, act in some heroic fashion on my own account? Within seconds—for I was a tolerably clear-headed small boy even in my extremity—I knew this to be nonsense. The situation held no scope for anything of the kind; I was a boy standing on the roof of a dining-room and not on a burning deck.

But at least there had come to me the idea of finding a role. In *Black Beauty* was there not somebody who rescued a cabby from an abyss of inebriety through the persistent timely tender of cups of coffee or perhaps cocoa? I considered this seriously, and saw that there would be considerable practical difficulties in applying the technique to my father, even supposing him at all disposed to submit to it. More promising seemed the stance of an Angel Child. For some months before going to school I had been provided with a governess who taught me my letters and numbers, and who was given to rewarding any progress I made by reading to me from a little book of stories strongly homiletic in character. I had thus heard of numerous angelic children adept at bringing quarrelsome servants or brothers or even parents in accord, or eliciting from tramps confessions of idleness, promises of amendment, and undertakings never again to neglect saying their prayers. I felt (not unreasonably) that, despite their appearance at the breakfast-table, my parents must be in large measure estranged as a consequence of the state of affairs that I had heard about on that terrible night. Perhaps I could do something about that. Perhaps I could be an Angel Child.

I started in as one at once. Tumbling down the spiral staircase, I went in search of my parents, and found them in a small lounge in which they frequently spent half-an-hour after breakfast. My father was reading *The Scotsman*, and my mother knitting some garment for my own wear. It was a lovely morning, I said, so might we not all go for a walk? Perhaps up to the Monument. There would be a splendid view.

They were surprised but—I thought—pleased. About my habit of solitary rambling I knew that they a little differed, my father judging it a reasonable sort of pleasure, and my mother believing it would be more 'natural' for me to be constantly seeking playmates among the other children at the hydro. But now once or twice a glance I caught between them worried me. Was it possible that they were not merely surpised by my unusual initiative, but *wondering*? Could it have occurred to them that I had been awake when I ought to have been asleep, and had as a consequence heard what was unfit for my ears? I think I felt obscurely that any awareness that they were taking a walk with an Angel Child might militate against the success of my operation. Nevertheless, I persevered. I managed to choose one of the broader paths, on which three could walk abreast. I managed to position myself between them, so that I could take a hand of each. I considered the possibility of myself pausing or halting for a moment as if to pick up and admire a particularly large fir cone, and in doing so slip my parents' hands each into other. But this, I decided, would be rushing things. We reached the Monument; we admired the view; my father pointed out in the distance a modest house once belonging to his grandfather, and told a story about this ancestor that I didn't really follow. Then we walked back to the hydro. It had been an uneventful expedition. Still, it had been a start.

But I got no further that day. After lunch my parents disappeared—mysteriously, because contrary to their habit. Had they sought, I wondered, some retired place in which my mother could renew her dire prognostication and my father make those horribly abject responses? The thought of it as perhaps a tediously reiterated scene made me chill all over, and at dinner the appearance of a favourite currant pudding failed to attract even a flicker of my interest. My mind was given wholly to a desperate searching for any means which an Angel Child might feasibly take to save an incipient drunkard from his doom. I thought, for instance, of persuading my father to climb with me unaccompanied to the battlements of the Monument, and there achieve a man-to-man talk, temperate and even worldly in tone, on the perils of alcohol in a general way. But, try as I would, it sounded hollow and unpersuasive on my inward ear.

My bedtime was pronounced, as it now invariably was, at half-past eight. Surprisingly, I went to sleep at once—only to wake up again at some unknown hour in darkness and what was still an empty room. My wakefulness at once became intolerable. It couldn't yet be what grown-ups for some reason called the small hours (weren't they, when occasionally I had encountered them in illness, eternities of a sort?). It couldn't even be midnight, or my parents would be in bed. I decided to read, since that would at least carry the pleasure of something forbidden at such an hour. I switched on my bedside light, knowing that I could instantly extinguish it at the sound of an opening door, and reached out for *Black Beauty*.

Black Beauty wasn't there, and I realized with dismay that I must have left it in that Reading Room. The dismay was acute, and for an odd and trivial reason. I have mentioned that it had been a prize at baby-school. Such a school might now be called a pre-prep. And because hitched to a proper prep which was in turn hitched to an august and heavily classical public school proper, even its prizes for near-infants were handsomely bound in full calf, with elaborately gilded and be-laurelled inscriptions in Latin and Greek on the front and back covers respectively. I somehow knew that this was pretentious and absurd on a silly little story about a talking horse, and I couldn't bear the thought of some unknown guest at the hydro discovering it, opening it, and finding my name under the word *Dux* on the inside. Desperate although the venture would be, I nerved myself to retrieve my property at once.

The desperateness proceeded from the fact that—here on the ground floor—I could get to the Reading Room only by passing the big room dedicated to badminton by day, and by night to the stupid games and charades and so forth which my father and mother were presumably goggling at now. To be detected prowling past its doors would be extremely unpleasant. Nevertheless, I scrambled out of bed and undertook the journey.

'*. . . softening of the brain . . .*'

Through a door slightly ajar I heard the words once more—and in my mother's voice. And then I heard my father's voice as well: the abject and maudlin voice. I am fairly sure it carried the truth of the situation to me instantly, and that the truth made me, at least for some instants, incapable of hearing anything more. What I next did hear was lukewarm applause, and then a penetrating whisper from some elderly man who must have been sitting near the door.

'As family entertainment, I call it in damned bad taste.'

And so it was. What I had listened to on that dreadful night had been nothing more than a rehearsal of one of my father's ploys for the discomfiting of what he regarded as a smug section of society. Probably the disappearance of my parents that afternoon had been to give a final polish to the wretched little playlet they had now presented: a kind of domesticated *Grand Guignol* affair. And that my mother had lent herself to it was an index of the extent to which my father dominated us.

Forgetting all about *Black Beauty*, I rushed back to Parlour 4, flung myself on my bed, and gave way to a passion of weeping. The relief was, of course, unspeakable—but so, obviously, was the sheer shock inherent in the thing. I must have wept unrestrainedly for some time, since eventually I was aware of my mother bending over me and murmuring soothing words.

'Was it a very bad dream, darling? But it's over now. For here I am, and here is your daddy, too. Now, go to sleep again.'

And there ends, I suppose, anything that can be called my story. But not of my wondering about the whole weird experience. Did it, in some 'unconscious' fashion, influence my later life in ways I cannot guess? Did I invent it all, and then, at some impenetrable level of the mind, come to transform fiction into fact? Even this I do not know. Professor Freud and his followers speak of screen memories, of fabrications which substitute themselves for authentic experiences not to be contemplated— and particularly of one which they call (a shade oddly) 'the primal scene'. In Parlour 4, I suppose, there may have been scope for my exposure to something of that kind.

There is one further thing that I remember, or seem to remember. It is the sense of having been *let down*. I believe that again I sulked for a time, simply because the opportunity of being an Angel Child had been denied me. This, if true, is perhaps the most shocking part of the whole thing. But I am uncertain about it. After all, I have been writing of events—or non-events—from very many years ago.

ANDRÉ

ANDRÉ NOW HAD a job. His mother was devout; the Curé said a good word for him; here he was as a functionary, a government official. The government, indeed, was of a local order, that Ville de Douarnenez not much known to the world beyond the bounds of this part of Brittany.

Still, at sixteen André had made a promising start. Although on a part-time basis, his employment ran to two stints a day, with overtime at pay-and-a-quarter every now and then. Promotion was always possible, or could at least be dreamed of. André had for long admired the youths—some of them no older than he was now—who worked, at a high speed that seemed entirely agreeable to them, on the lumbering mechanized dust-carts which beneath an imperiously flashing yellow light made their jerky way through the narrow streets of Douarnenez and even of sleepy Tréboul itself. It was exciting merely to watch the powerful revolving jaws of these monsters. They crushed and swallowed whatever you cared to pitch into them, and their servants, although possibly drafted on the work willy-nilly under some law for ameliorating juvenile unemployment, were exhilarated by their task.

A cart seldom came quite to a halt; at its rear were minute protruding platforms upon which the young men leapt as it moved—thence to lean out and forward scanning the lines of waiting dustbins ahead with all the fixed regard of charioteers intent upon the goal, drinking the wind of their own speed. They vied with one another in spotting on the footpaths promisingly indigestible objects to chuck within the hungry maw of their voracious master. Every now and then one of the lads, after a swift precautionary glance around, would hurl in not merely the contents of a rubbish bin but the rubbish bin itself. The monster would falter for a moment, take as it were a deep pneumatic breath, and crumple and engulf the offering as if it were no more than a matchbox, or a paper carton thrown down in the street after its last Gauloise had been smoked. And the willing slaves of the monster, their torsos glittering with sweat and their muscles in fine trim for display, would utter triumphant shouts as if themselves accomplishing a prodigious feat of strength. These paeans they mingled with pleasantries of an innocently indecent sort.

For André such companionable jollity still lay in an uncertain future. His present labour was solitary, and the receptacle he served was not a mechanical giant but a black plastic sack. Emptied into a larger sack several times in the course of each stint, it had to last a week before a fresh sack (to the value of perhaps ten centimes) would be issued to him by the responsible superintendent. By that time a good many small rents would have appeared in the current sack, occasioned by the more jagged objects which unthinking persons had left littering the beach.

Such was André's employment. He was, of sorts, a beachcomber, although one toiling without hope of private profit. Once in the early morning when almost nobody was abroad, and once in the late afternoon when, alike above and below the tide-line, a scattering of sun-dazed gluttons still lay inconveniently around, André traversed first the big and then the little beach to and fro on innumerable straight lines, stooping every few feet or yards to gather up with one hand the miscellaneous rubbish which he then transferred to the sack he trailed behind him with the other. It was monotonous work, and when the monotony was disturbed it was because something more than commonly disagreeable had to be dealt with. But André was conscientious, and if he sometimes had the bold thought that a little spade, or long-handled pincers, or those handsome black and yellow *gants industriels* issued to the young men on the big rubbish carts would improve his lot, he judged that an application for anything of the kind would be adversely regarded by those powers to whom he owed the favour of being employed at all. So he carried on as he was, and habit eventually dulled his sensibilities in this direction.

André lived in the upper part of Tréboul, midway along the little Passage des Sirènes. It was a modest dwelling, but satisfactory in that, simply by jumping on his bicycle at its door, he could project himself without so much as touching the handle-bars straight down the rue des Professeurs Curie, past the splendours of the Centre Cure Marine and the Grand Hôtel of Tréboul and the Universe, so as to arrive like a bullet at his place of employment. This conduced to punctuality. But to his mother the house's main satisfactoriness lay in the fact that from its garret window her son could edify himself with a glimpse of Monsieur Saint Yves. If indeed the battered devotional object perched above its massive granite steps *was* Saint Yves. For, although the monument seemed miraculously to have left off crumbling centuries ago, it was not before any indisputable identification had become impossible.

There were those who held the figure to be that of Saint Anne, a Breton princess who, miraculously transported to Nazareth, there gave birth to the Virgin Mary—having accomplished which exalted task she returned to Brittany, where she was subsequently paid a family visit by our Saviour. But an old woman had told André of her grandmother's declaring that the abraded saint was neither Saint Anne nor Saint Yves but Saint Tugen, since long ago he had held aloft what was distinguishably a key. And any key, if touched by Saint Tugen's key, would infallibly drive away mad dogs—Saint Tugen being in fact one of the most useful of Brittany's specialist saints.

André liked this interpretation of the statue. Indeed, secretly in the single pocket of his truncated jeans he carried a little key of his own, which when quite small and at dead of night he had contrived after some scrambling to apply notionally to this long-since vanished part of the monument. Although he would have been reluctant to confess it, he still placed some reliance on this key. On both his beaches he frequently had to deal with the undesired offerings of Tréboul's wandering dogs. They were decent enough dogs in a normal condition—but it was a time at which *la rage* was said to be advancing like the first covert scouts of an invading army from Normandy. About these dogs André had another of his venturesome ideas. By the entrance to Tréboul's public garden hung the representation of a wholly endearing dog and the injunction:

Faîtes-lui faire ses
besoins hors du JARDIN!
Les ENFANTS y jouent

Why not have similar notices at both beaches—simply reading *des PLAGES* instead of *du JARDIN*? But this, too, André thought that it might be judged overweening to suggest prematurely to the municipal authorities. All the same, it would be quite fun.

As the season advanced and the number of visitors to Tréboul mounted, André's labours were inevitably more prolonged. In a limited—and sometimes disturbing—way, they became more interesting as well. The abandoned cigarette packets were not invariably quite empty; newspapers cast negligently away could be read only by persons conversant with alien tongues; occasionally bottles had been smashed in a disobliging and dangerous fashion before being cast aside, so that their late contents were to be arrived at only from embossed inscriptions or from scraps of labels blotched by spindrift or dew. But, also, here and there in the more secluded places lay flaccid testimonies of amorous enterprises achieved by night. These, to be dealt with only in the most gingerly manner, drew André's thoughts in a natural but also a disquieting direction. He possessed an adequate theoretical knowledge of what you did to girls, but had made no start at all with its practical application. In this he would quite soon be in a humiliating minority (or so, at least, he had been persuaded) among his male contemporaries. Those happy *balayeurs* on the rubbish carts, with some of whom he was on chattering, joking terms: he thought of them all as sinning and confessing (if they still went in for that) and sinning again as briskly as they hurled those bins at work and swam and dived at play.

Visualizing these felicities with an envy that he knew to be entirely in order, he yet nursed an obscure feeling that there might be something lacking in them. He had no idea what. It was a guessed-at region, this, to which his only access was through the doors of the local cinema, on the flickering screen of which much ado was made of passion apparently of a soul-searching, soul-shattering, but ultimately ennobling sort. Whether he could measure up to that sort of thing, he didn't know at all.

He took to lingering on the increasingly crowded beaches through long afternoons, carefully in a near-nakedness so as to avoid being conspicious. The spectacle was astonishing. Prone or supine, flat on bellies or bottoms, inert, faintly twitching, restlessly wriggling, there sprawled acre upon acre of bronzed human flesh which rendered paler the pale sand beneath it. Flashes of bright colour here and there were parasols, miniature tents, towels, skimpy *cache-sexe* mini-garments. A ceaseless hubbub blended the shouts of children and the jabber of grown-ups with the unresting sibilation of the sea. André had no idea where all these people came from, or what was their station in life. He rather supposed that most of them were enormously rich; were in every direction as affluent as those weird Americans whose serialized fortunes you could follow on television in a café over a lingering mug of chocolate.

But Jules laughed at this. Jules, a schoolfellow of André's, had landed himself a job in the Grand Hôtel. At the moment he was a simple *plongeur* pretty well round the clock, but at any time he might graduate to a white jacket and the carrying of clean plates into the restaurant and dirty ones out of it. Meanwhile, he was keeping his eyes open, and reporting his conclusions to his friend.

'Grocers,' Jules said, as the two lay side by side on the sand. 'French, Dutch, English—but little bourgeois cattle one and all. This man is a coal-merchant, and that one—but in a small way—tins stinking meat for cats. For the whole lot it's their annual blow-out, their bloody spree. They rejoice for the time at having other people to run about emptying their slops.'

'They don't belong, then, to the fashionable world?'

'Of course not, dunderhead. Your fashionable world wouldn't give a fart for the lot of them. Except for having a sou or two more in their pockets, they're just like you and me. But we give a bow and a bob, we open a door, we say "Good morning, ladies" as if we loved the bitches, and perhaps a few centimes come our way. It's life.'

André found this information disillusioning.

'So it's like that?' he said. 'They're all of a piece?'

'As like as a turd's like a turd.'

'But they're not, Jules.' André's own professional knowledge came into play here. 'There are turds and turds.'

'Understood! And—just sometimes—there is here also the exceptional thing. I mean at our hotel. It is, one has to grant, as tolerable a hotel as this wretched flea-bitten corner of France can show. And, just occasionally, the people of a superior sort will come. Not many. And always couples.'

'Couples?'

'Fornication in a corner, my good André. Rich, and even perhaps of good family, well brought up. They come because nobody of their own acquaintance will be here too, to spot them in a compromising situation.' Jules paused for a moment. 'The English,' he then went on, 'speak of "a dirty week-end". But we French exhaust ourselves less easily. In and out, in and out for a fortnight—and then look around elsewhere. That's us.'

André ceased to listen, since Jules's chatter was drifting into routine. Instead, he gazed with unaccustomed reflectiveness at the scene before him. The further shore of the Bay of Douarnenez had disappeared within a haze of heat, so that the horizon was a great arc of blue against which, so distant as to seem immobile, a single cruising yacht could be seen. But near at hand was a maze of rapid movement as the innumerable *planches à voile* of the younger holiday-makers composed beneath their multicoloured sails a kaleidoscopic harlequinade of zig-zag or arrow-like motions. They tussled with what appeared to be an unnatural battle of the winds—these intrepid wind-surfers—and appeared able to move simultaneously in parallel but diametrically opposed directions, like jousting knights charging one another at the tilt. Abruptly dismounted ever and again as their sails flopped over and lay awash on the surface of the sea, the riders were for all the world like warriors unhorsed by the enemy, yet practised in heaving their steeds upright again and renewing the fray.

This martial reverie drew André's thoughts to ancient things imperfectly understood in lessons at school. Many were of dire conflicts and grim revenges. For example, centred on that now peaceful if tourist-crammed island just concealed on his right hand beyond the Môle du Biron there had been the evil La Fontenelle, the devastator of all Brittany, who had ended his days as a huddle of broken and bloodied bones on King Henri's wheel.

That lesson had been disagreeable, and André glanced at Jules in order to converse about something more cheerful. But Jules had fallen asleep, which is a proper enough thing to do on a vacant summer afternoon. So André resumed his study of the scene. There was a second arc, this time a concave one and demarcated by little scarlet buoys, on the barely ruffled sea. The wind-surfers had to keep outside this arc, since these nearer waters were reserved for the swimmers, the young men and older children diving from the tall *plongeoir*, the paddling infants and their anxious mamas. All these people still made a great deal of noise—noise against which the little rippling waves directed their lulling murmur in vain.

On the beach, however, there were plenty of sleepers besides Jules. It was as if the sun, hammering down on their near-nakedness, had knocked them out. Those that weren't asleep read *livres de poche*, tickled each other's spines with feathers or caressed each other's behinds, munched *petits pains au chocolat*. Although the Mayor of Douarnenez owned impressive convictions about public decency, and itemized them in the lengthy *arrêts* placarded here and there along the seaboard, he had failed to convince many of the sun-bathing ladies that more than a few centimetres of their mystery need be concealed from the general view. But although André's eyes duly lingered on the naked breasts of these alien creatures, he was not confident that they excited him quite as much as they should. He would have preferred, he saw, to this abundant and gratuitous but disregarding display a more restricted, a more gradual and reciprocal intimacy achieved by some manly persistence of his own. He wondered whether it might be possible to discuss this with Jules on a serious rather than a prescriptively ribald note. But Jules continued to slumber, and presently André went home.

It was midway through the holiday period that Monsieur Hochedur appeared. He didn't introduce himself and he didn't shake hands. André learnt his name only from one of the men at the *poste de secours*: unfortunate fellows who, it was said, promptly lost their job if a kid got drowned within the *baignade surveillée* in the vast bay. A small boy who invariably accompanied Monsieur Hochedur, presumably his son, was called Alexandre.

The point about M. Hochedur—and it would surely have made at least a nodding acquaintance the proper thing—was that there he was every morning, moving slowly up and down the beach and doing almost exactly what André did. The difference between them was that M. Hochedur operated a metal-detector. It took André a little time to understand the functioning of this instrument. You might have called it a saucer at the end of a stick, and up from it there ran a short flex that ended in a little plug in Monsieur Hochedur's left ear. M. Hochedur—much as if he were an Indian holy man concerned to sweep beetles and the like aside and into safety as he walked—swayed the saucer gently to and fro before his path and just above the level of the sand. Every now and then he would come to a halt and point at a spot immediately in front of him. Whereupon the stupid little Alexandre (for André felt him to be that) would stoop, scrabble, and unearth some minute object which he then transferred to a pouch hanging at his father's side.

It was, of course, Jules who explained this novel form of beachcombing.

'Mostly,' Jules said, 'it is small change tumbled from the pocket—a thing likely to happen during the embrace. It may be a bunch of keys—surely a find of little account—or even the strip one rips away from the top of a bottle of Coke—which is of less account still. But there will be chains, bracelets, small articles of jewellery from time to time. Or in his folly the man may think to discover treasure buried by pirates, or by guerillas devastating the country during the troubles of the League.' Jules, like André, still commanded scraps of the learning imparted to him at school.

'And what one finds, one keeps?'

'Evidently.'

'But, Jules, I have myself never found anything like that—except the little seals off the Cokes.'

'It may be because yours are superficial labours, my brave fellow. The electric eye goes deeper. It is the reason of its being, that.'

'On the same beach day after day!' André was suddenly scornful. 'It makes no sense at all.'

'Nearly everyone is wealthier than we are, André. But not all have even our modest sagacity.'

André, who had no talent for philosophical remarks, said nothing more. But he decided to dislike M. Hochedur. After a fashion, surely, the man was queering his pitch.

The girl's arrival—or André's first awareness of her—happened on the following day. Nothing spectacular was to come of it: certainly not drama of the heart-searing sort so freely available in the cinema. The setting, however, was worthy of the high canons of romance. The dawn had come up like the first bars of a symphony barely breaking in upon the long silence of the night, and André had been at work before any further orchestration began. Only because it was faintly moving could the blue-grey sea be distinguished from the sky—and the movement itself was so gentle, so reluctant-seeming, that the wide stretch of water spread before Tréboul seemed not yet to have shed the lassitude of the dark. The low waves stole upon the beach in fine, dark lines without a hint of foam, but in a curve of the bay lying beneath the direct rays of the risen sun the barely luminous surface of the sea turned to a brilliant and glittering ellipse as of liquid gems. On the nearer sand, humped and pitted like a bleak mountainous region viewed from high in air, André's shadow was still twelve metres long.

There was scarcely a living creature around. The gulls, whose multitudinous imprints had almost obliterated naked or plimsoll-shod footsteps on the sand, had departed out to sea, or were comfortably perched on the high *plongeoir* within the bathing area. M. Hochedur and Alexandre had not yet arrived; only from the small van of *La Surf School Bihan* two men and a girl were unloading boards and sails in preparation for the first breeze of the day. It was like an empty stage in a theatre where a scattered audience was nevertheless already assembled, since from among the dark trees of the Bois d'Isis, on the hilly ground here above the bay, the windows in the steeply-pitched, grey-slated roofs of a score of white-walled villas gazed down, Argus-eyed, upon the scene. And every now and then as André turned to retraverse his uneventful round he would see in the Grand Hôtel a blind going up, shutters thrown back. So there in a sense was a gathering audience too.

The girl was certainly a guest from the hotel, early abroad through some stir of impatience or curiosity at which it was impossible to guess. Perched on a sea-wall in the first warmth of the sun, she glanced without curiosity at M. Hochedur when he did turn up to start his absurd electronic fossicking. But as André himself drew a little nearer (yet no closer than he felt propriety permitted) she quickly lowered her head, produced a book, turned a page. The effect of this on André was strange. He found himself astounded. The girl was aware of him! It couldn't be put other than like that.

So in the middle of his dull scavenging André was thrown into confusion. He wished he was in his Sunday clothes. Then instantly, and more sensibly, he wished he was in almost no clothes at all. He was a boy proud, whether justly or not, of his ability at certain games. He believed that his virility would prove to be something beyond the average when at length the specific challenge to it turned up. But he had given only cursory thought as to whether his whole person was agreeable to the eye. The tall looking-glass in his mother's room, before which he had on several occasions posed his nude body when she was safely out of the house, had assured him that it was probably so. Yet this, which seemed to lie in the field of mere aesthetics, he had seldom troubled himself with again. Now, and in an instant, the question had presented itself anew. It was as if, entirely to his surprise, Great Creating Nature herself had taken him by the scruff of the neck and given him his orders. How otherwise was it that he found himself suddenly behind a convenient bathing box, stripping off the single garment that left him naked to the hips and from the thighs?

There was, of course, nothing to occasion alarm in this action. The morning was already turning warm, and within a few hours those human pelts coloured like the darkest honey would again be almost obscuring the beach. Nevertheless, circumspection now became André's main concern. As he resumed his labours he allowed himself not a glance at the girl, who as a consequence grew enchantingly beautiful in his imagination as mere minutes went by. And he kept his distance, even traversing the same path several times and to no further effective scavenging at all in order that this might be so. But his motions became considered in a new way. He had discovered long ago that as he perpetually stooped and stooped to gather his scraps of rubbish it made for ease from time to time a little to elevate behind him one leg or the other. Almost unconsciously, he was now importing a certain grace into this manoeuvre. Like the Egyptian ladies in Shakespeare's play, André made his bends adornings.

He had nearly cleared the larger beach, and the girl was still there: perched on the low wall, now turning again the pages of her book, and now gazing out over the bay, on which the first scudding *planches à voile* were beginning to appear. M. Hochedur was still at work too—quite close by, so that his criss-crossings with André were like a slow-motion parody of the swiftly converging and parting wind-surfers themselves. There was something ridiculous in this, and André suspected that the girl found it to be so. Stealing a glance at her, he once or twice thought to catch a corresponding glance directed upon him.

Boldness, just a little boldness, was surely admissible in such a situation.

He applied himself with a quickened pace to the strip of sand between them, so that soon it became a matter of metres only. He was abreast of her, and for the first time looked at her other than covertly. It was to find that she was doing the same by him. He heard himself saying, '*Bonjour, Madame*'. '*Madame*' was perhaps a little silly, but he judged it to be more courteous than '*Mademoiselle*'.

'Oh, good morning—*bonjour*.' The girl—and she *was* amazingly beautiful—had been taken by surprise. But she didn't seem displeased. She was, of course, a foreigner. André had known she must be that. Had it not been from Ireland that King Mark's destined bride, Iseult, was companioned by Tristan, and on the voyage to Brittany that the two had drunk the fatal potion? Had not this very shore been part of Mark's kingdom of Cornouaille? André, whose schooling had been coincident with a burgeoning of Breton nationalist sentiment, knew all about that. And the strangely heady memory of the lovers' story came back to him now.

The girl had smiled at him, although with an unlingering glance. Then she closed her book, slipped from the wall, and walked back to the Grand Hôtel. Yet certainly her father could not be one of those who tinned bad meat for cats. Perhaps she was really a princess, just as Iseult had been.

On the following morning she made no appearance. André, now deeply in love's toils without quite knowing it, waited and watched much as the young Troilus must have waited and watched for Cressida as dawn paled the camp-fires of the Achaeans. There was only the detestable M. Hochedur effecting his humiliating travesty (as it might be felt to be) of the unassuming but necessary and sensible labour upon which André himself was engaged. M. Hochedur was moreover in a bad temper. He twice slapped the face of the miserable little Alexandre in a merely wanton way, and whereas he had never admitted any awareness of André's presence before, he now treated him to an ugly scowl whenever their paths crossed. Conceivably he was feeling that this particular El Dorado had exhausted itself and that he ought by this time to have moved on to another beach.

It was then that the odd thing happened.

André was fully clad again—in a T-shirt much admired by his mother, which bore on its breast the injunction *En avant Citroën!* Some consciousness newly born in him made the boy aware of a demeaning slant to this—for why should he thus advertise a chunk of hardware he was unlikely ever to possess? So perhaps he wasn't himself in a very good temper either. With unwonted clumsiness he sometimes fumbled in his picking up of the previous day's squalid litter, and it was because of this that at one point his fingers went quite deep into the sand and came upon some small, hard object buried there. He brought it to the light. It was a woman's ring, and he gazed at it for a moment unbelievingly. As he had told Jules, he had never come on anything valuable throughout his now considerable professional experience. Set in a band of white metal, slender but curiously heavy, was a single large and brilliant gem.

'Ten francs.'

André became aware that M. Hochedur had halted beside him, that the man's eyes were fixed on the ring, and that he had uttered these words with an objectionable lack of ceremony.

'Pardon?' André said.

'The thing's a mere trinket. But I'll give you ten francs for it.' M. Hochedur held out an imperious hand. 'Show it to me.'

This command André, no doubt foolishly, obeyed. So M. Hochedur took the ring, and at once afforded evidence of a disposition to appropriate it. But now, as it happened, two citizens of respectable standing, who for reasons of health were taking an early-morning stroll on the beach, had paused to observe the small incident. M. Hochedur, thinking better of thus forcing the issue, handed the ring back to André.

'Almost worthless,' he said. 'Still, twenty francs.'

This abrupt doubling of what in André's regard was already a substantial sum of money was a mistake. It alarmed him a little, and at the same time it seriously offended him. Quite unaccountably as yet, the ring had become something not to chaffer over.

'But I think not,' he said decisively, and turned and walked away. Then he dropped the ring into his pocket—thus lodging it beside the key that would have touched Saint Tugen's key had Saint Tugen's key survived to be touched.

So did the ring bring André luck? It is a question hard to answer—as are all questions to the resolving of which some definition of happiness is essential. Certainly the girl almost at once began to appear again. Perhaps, after thought, she had judged it pleasurable to include in her holiday routine a glance at—even a brief word with—the boy who cleaned up the beach. But she didn't make anything of the kind emphatic. It couldn't have been said that she was approachable in any improper way. Sometimes her thoughts seemed far off, and she would stroll past André on the still almost empty beach disregardingly. At other times she would ravishingly say 'Hallo', and her eyes would take in not merely his shy smile but his whole body. This turned him giddy. It perplexed him that he didn't start imagining things—evolving fantasies in which unbelievable intimacies took place. But nothing of the sort happened to trouble the long enchanted moment in which he lived. And some things that had formerly amused him now seemed impossibly crude.

Of this there was one striking instance. André's way home from his labour was up that steep rue des Professeurs Curie, where it was necessary to get off his bike and trudge. It had become his habit to pause half-way at a spot where a small expanse of tussocky grass occasionally afforded an odd diversion. For here some of the rowdier young people of the neighbourhood would often be at horseplay of a peculiar sort. In particular, three lads of his own age or a little older, together with a hoyden of a girl, had evolved a burlesque kind of fighting with, seemingly, no holds barred. One saw such antics at circuses or on TV, and this quartet had worked quite hard on them, so that what was on view was a very fair imitation of Kung Fu or some such outlandish thing—with various indecencies thrown in for luck. Motionlessly challenging at one moment, the four would be all whirling activity, savage intent, the next. What they had chiefly mastered was a trick of turning full circle on the heel with incredible rapidity—lashing out, feinting, ducking, jabbing the while. The chief victim was the girl. One lout would trip her, pitch her to the ground; another would grab a leg and with a series of mere flicks transform her into a species of garden roller. But in a moment she would be on her feet—laughing wildly, kicking out at her aggressors with a seemingly murderous force finely calculated to fall just short of the groin. And the louts too would be laughing loudly, since part of the fun was to create a tremendous row. André had been finding all this—not least its crass sexuality—highly entertaining, and even stimulating in an agreeable way. Now he judged it horrid, and austerely passed it by. The eternal womanly was leading him higher.

But he had moments of disillusion, or at least lucidity, and in these it would occur to him that the girl's holiday must end and she must simply go away. Cautiously by way of Jules (who was amused) he instigated mundane inquiries about her. Had she parents, brothers, sisters? Were they rich—the kind of people who would have yachts, many large cars, beautiful clothes, costly jewels?

'By no means.' Jules from amid his pots and pans had been developing—or so he believed—a flair for refined social discriminations. 'Of substance, yes; and of good family, it may be, in their country's fashion. But rich, not. More manners at the table than money in the bank.' Jules paused to admire his own power of epigram. 'And they leave—papa, mama, a younger brother—at the end of the week.'

André was dismayed, but at least he was learning something. 'Supposing,' he asked, 'one of them lost some costly thing: a fine camera, a necklace, a gold watch. What would they do?'

'Fuss about it, of course. Enquiries would be made, a notice would be put up, the *patron* would begin suspecting one or another of us, and questioning the rest.'

'But there has been nothing of the sort?'

'Nothing at all.'

André was reassured. It was not the girl herself who had lost the ring. Had it been so, merely to restore it to her would have been a joy. But he now nursed—no doubt culpably—a far more splendid design. He would make a present of the ring, an offering tendered with deep respect! But there was ground he still had to make certain of.

'Those others you spoke about,' he said. 'The hugely rich. Are there at present any of them in the hotel?'

'Lately, yes. But they are now gone away. People of the jet-set sort.' Jules was coming to command a good deal of *frangláis* of this order. 'Their morals were bad. Here on these very beaches they would, some of them, misconduct themselves in the night.'

'Jules, supposing such people, so engaged, lost such a thing as we have spoken of—a watch, or it might be a ring—would they, as you say those English would, create a fuss about it?'

'But no. It would mean nothing to them: the object and such value as it had. They would be discreet, and keep mum.'

So that was it; that was the explanation of the ring. André's path was clear, and there was no time to lose. He acted next day.

Soon after his arrival on the beach the girl was there, carrying her book in a rather perfunctory fashion—much as a priest might carry his breviary on holiday. And again she smiled and nodded. With his heart in his mouth, André walked straight up to her.

'Good morning, Mademoiselle. You leave us soon?'

'Tomorrow morning, I'm afraid.' The girl was surprised: amused, perhaps, but not startled. They were, after all, acquaintances already, after a fashion.

'May I, then, offer you a small present?' And André, resolutely if in a shaking hand, held out the ring.

'Oh, but really . . .' She was now frankly confused, and had momentarily lapsed from her schoolgirl's French into English. 'But it is too kind of you and I don't a bit deserve it. So, please, no!'

But something in André sensed that this was not a true negative. Her eyes were signalling that her heart was touched.

She liked him as a girl should like a boy, and he asked for nothing more. For a moment, at least, his bliss was entire.

'As a souvenir of Tréboul,' he said. 'It is nothing in itself. A trinket merely.' He had remembered M. Hochedur's depreciating word.

'Then, thank you very much. I shall remember Tréboul—and, of course, yourself as well.' She had taken the ring. Conscious, perhaps, of the need to be gracious, she gave it an admiring glance, but refrained from attempting to slip it on a finger. And suddenly André knew there was something more that had to pass his lips.

'I love you,' he said—and without a moment's pause turned and walked away. He didn't look back. It was over. He knew that he would never see his princess, the English girl, again. Already, had he known it, she was looking at the ring once more, and now a little strangely. Her people weren't rich, but her mother's small jewel-case, at least, was familiar to her. Was it possible . . . ?

The girl quickened her pace back to the Grand Hôtel. Her first thought was to consult her father, tell him of this almost alarming sequel to a very simple sort of love-liking, fleeting love-liking, for a handsome peasant boy. But as she studied the ring once more, the full awkwardness of the thing dawned on her. The ring wasn't a trinket by a very long way, and her father wouldn't be the prudent lawyer he was if he didn't find it wise to investigate what had occurred. He would say no word to suggest that the boy must be a thief. But that would be his thought. And he wouldn't countenance for a moment inaction before a situation whereby his daughter, after however bizarre a fashion, had conceivably become the recipient of stolen goods. Through one agency or another, unbearable inquiries would be made.

She stopped in her tracks. She wasn't frightened. She knew very well that there was little danger of her being hauled before some magistrate and interrogated. But it wasn't so with the boy. They would be after him like a shot. As she realized this, her embarrassment, her mere distress, turned into a kind of horror in face of life's treacheries. Perhaps the boy *had* stolen the ring—the boy who had spoken those words to her and at once turned away. She knew nothing about him—or only that he was plainly a penniless lad, hired for some pittance to collect rubbish from a beach. But he had said *that*. And he had meant it.

Suddenly the girl walked on, and at a quicker pace, now making not for the hotel but for the rocky promontory at the far end of the beach: the spot where the Germans had built their gun-emplacements. These had been levelled to the ground, but at one point a long concrete platform still jutted out sheer above the sea. To this the girl walked more slowly—her mind being made up and now curiously at ease. Reaching the verge, she paused for a moment, and then gently cast the ring into the secure oblivion of Douarnenez Bay.

André was disconsolate for weeks. The season was drawing to its close, and with it his job. He would be among Brittany's thousands of unemployed. Perhaps he would chum up with the louts and their trollop on that tussocky grass, and learn Kung Fu.

The sky grew full of cloud, and the breakers full of sand. At the *poste de secours* a brown pennant had replaced a green: *Baignade dangereuse*. Even experienced wind-surfers were in trouble: the speed-boats guarding them busy giving one or another a humiliating tow to land. The children's trampolines had been folded away; the *École de Natation*, the *Piscina Nausicaa*, the *Club Micky Éducation Physique* had all gone out of business. Autumn was over everything, and one knew that the Atlantic raved outside the western straits of France.

What had André achieved? Nothing at all. Even the Mayor of Douarnenez had got ahead of him in one important regard. Instead of the small joke he had himself thought up there had belatedly appeared a large placard announcing:

Plage interdite aux chiens

And a day came when there were no human beings on the beach at all. There were only half-a-dozen dogs.

PIPKIN GROVE

IT WAS A very ordinary evening at the Thimbles. Young Harold Thimble had taken himself off on his motor-bike to Youth Redeployment, as he regularly did on Mondays and Thursdays. Harold was on the dole, and Youth Redeployment was providing the gen. that might get him into some vaguely adumbrated venture in electronics. Or so Harold said. His mum believed him and would remark—quite truly—that Harold had always been having ideas, and that Youth Redeployment was one of them. His dad, who disliked ideas but felt he knew the world, said Youth Redeployment was probably the pub, or perhaps it was riding round up to no special good with a bunch of hippies. Harold's sister, Samantha, never said anything much. Samantha had managed to train as a hair-stylist, and now worked in a unisex place called Follicles. After her day's artistic striving she was sitting by the fire with a nice book: the previous week's issue of *Modern Brides*, which she had brought home from the saloon. Albert Thimble, the master of the house, was also reading, and had got to page 3 of *The Sun*. Chummy, the Thimbles' cat, snoozing on the hearth-rug, gently wagged the very tip of her tail. It was all entirely normal and innocent—or at least it seemed to be. From scenes like these spring an ordered society and the repose of governments.

Perhaps a shade reluctantly, Albert Thimble turned on from page 3 to page 4. He frowned slightly, as if he had come on something that perplexed him. Glancing up from his paper, he saw that his wife, who had been pouring out cups of tea, was for some reason rejecting one cup and taking another from the shelf. He looked at his daughter and the cat, his frown deepening. Samantha and Chummy were yawning simultaneously, so that it would have been impossible to tell which of them had caught the impulse from the other. Mr Thimble put down his paper.

'And now,' he said abruptly, 'there's going to be a terrible crash.'

Mrs Thimble placed the teapot back on the kitchen table.

Samantha glanced incuriously at her father and returned to her book, from which she had just gathered that an average wedding costs £1,500, not counting the never-never. Then, minutes later and without warning—only it was precisely *not* without warning—there was the sudden roar of a tremendous explosion. The whole house shook. Tea spurted from the spout of the teapot. Dust which oughtn't to have been there, but which perhaps lurked on valences and the tops and backs of picture-frames, rose and eddied round the light-bulbs. Chummy had arched herself and bristled like a cat in a strip cartoon.

A hundred years earlier, or thereabout, people like the Thimbles might have thought of anarchists, prowling London in inky cloaks and big black hats, bearing before them bombs like footballs emitting a tiny curl of smoke to show they were in business. Mrs Thimble remembered the blitz, and now she thought of it. Samantha, more up to date, saw that they hadn't, all three plus Chummy, been reduced to dirty marks on a wall, so at least they hadn't been nuked by the Russians. Then Mrs Thimble exclaimed, 'the I.R.A!' and felt she had found the answer. Of course, the I.R.A. went, on the whole, for prestige localities in the West End, not for unpretentious South London suburbs like Plumstead. But they were said to have inconspicuous houses all over the place, and to use them for manufacturing everything from block-busters to what the police liked to call incendiary devices. Sometimes they had an accident, and one of these houses went up with a bang. Mrs Thimble said that for some time she'd had an eye on comings and goings at Number 34 in their own street. So that must be it. The explosion must have been at Number 34. They were lucky it hadn't been nearer their own Number 14

'Terrorists,' Mrs Thimble said, not uncomfortably. 'As bad as that Goering and his Luftwaffy, they're coming to be. But you knew about *him*. That it was what-for for all of us, I mean, if our boys didn't stop him. But who knows anything about these Irish and what they're after? I don't. Let them alone, I say, and they mayn't come worrying quiet folk in Plumstead. Who lives in 34, I ask you? Not Mrs Thatcher.'

These political reflections didn't interest Samantha, who had simply returned to *Modern Brides*. But her father, although accepting his wife's theories that it had been Number 34 and no business of theirs, was plainly perturbed. It didn't seem to occur to him to go out into the street and investigate—not even when an urgent wailing of sirens and clangour of bells told that police cars and fire engines and ambulances were arriving in Pipkin Grove. And when at length he had something to say, it was haltingly and to an odd effect.

'I've known it before,' Albert Thimble said.

'Of course you have, Albert.' Mrs Thimble was impatient. 'That Goering——'

'Nothing to do with Goering, you old cow.' Mr Thimble made use of this endearment only when something more than commonly vexatious had occurred. 'Thinking a string of things have all happened before. Turning over from a bit of cheesecake and finding something about Albion Rovers. And then your fiddling with those cups. And Samantha and the cat both yawning after that. And then——'

'Shock,' Mrs Thimble said with authority. 'You're suffering from shock. They can take you into hospital for that, and give you the electricity, as like as not. So you'd better have a care.'

Not unnaturally, this lurid prediction further disturbed her husband.

'Shock to hell,' he said. 'But it's true I don't feel right in myself. I'll step out and take a breath of air.' This was Albert's common formula when he was prompted to drop into the local. 'And I'll let you know what's what.'

Mr Thimble hadn't been gone for ten minutes when a rapid series of quite small explosions announced that his son Harold had got home on his Yamaha. And he burst in some excitement into the kitchen.

'36,' he said. 'One of those gas things. The stuff builds up like it might be in the cellar—and there's a flash and the whole house goes sky-high. Just nothing left of 36. But one poor bugger—or the top half of one poor bugger, it looks like—decorating the chimney-pots of 38.'

'Disgusting!' Samantha said. She had glanced up briefly from *Modern Brides* to deliver this judgement.

'Well, just think—only gas!' There was a tinge of disappointment in Mrs Thimble's voice. 'But it's always happening, isn't it?'

'Nothing of the sort,' Harold Thimble said. 'When it does happen the papers play it up like mad. There'll be reporters and photographers out there now. But a year can go by, and it doesn't happen to one in a million houses in the land.' Harold paused. 'If that,' he added, rather as one who has consulted a highly refined computer in his head. 'Houses struck by lightning, and houses bashed into by runaway Juggernauts: there's more of them by a long way than there is of those gas affairs. Anyone who doesn't know that is ignorant.'

'Ignorant yourself,' Samantha said. Contradicting her brother often came to Samantha rather in the manner of a reflex action. 'Don't listen to him,' she added to her mother, '—him that can't as much as get a job to clear dog-shit from the pavements.'

'That isn't nice, Samantha.' Mrs Thimble always tried to insist on some refinement in the home. 'But, Harold, it took your father all funny, and now he's off to the Leather Bottle.'

'How do you mean, Mum, all funny?'

'Feeling that everything that was happening had happened before. Seeing one of those vulgar photos in his paper as if they'd printed the same one twice. And then the same way with Albion Rovers, and me and some teacups, and then Samantha and Chummy—all like it had been in the past, see? And then——'

'Oh, that!' Harold was contemptuous. 'He's told me about that more than once. He's susceptible like. Nothing in it.'

'What do you mean, susceptible?'

'Yes, susceptible!' Samantha echoed, and this time she tossed *Modern Brides* away from her. 'Talk English, Harold, for Christ's sake.'

'Then I'll try to explain.' Harold's tone suggested the patience of a devoted teacher confronting a batch of ESN infants. 'There's your conscious awareness like. Right, Mum?'

'My what?'

'Your conscious awareness. Somewhere inside your head there's a kind of TV screen, isn't there? With everything that goes on in front of you showing up on it just as it takes place. You know? And sounds as well, just as on the box. Smells, too.'

'Smells?' Mrs Thimble queried disapprovingly.

'And touch. Ever heard of the feelies, Mum? You might be putting out a hand and stroking the bloody cat. And there it all is in this consciousness—you know?—all that's happening in front of you here and now. See? But behind this conscious bit of your mind there's something else: a kind of lumber-room where you've stowed away all the old stuff that's no longer of use to you.'

'Harold, you're going a bit deep, aren't you? You must have been reading a book.' Mrs Thimble spoke as a nice-minded woman might do if constrained to comment upon some demeaning solitary indulgence.

'Well, I do, Mum. I do read books.' Harold's air suggested honest candour before such a charge. 'There's no harm in a few books. They're natural.'

'I'm not against education, Harold. It can be a wonderful thing. Your Uncle Ned—he's educated. And now with his own business, and something in the bank.'

'This isn't education. It's just thinking something out. We're talking about memory, see?'

'Memory, Harold?'

'This lumber-room. Every now and then you rummage in it—you know?—and fish out something you need again. Like it might be whether you've already fed the bloody cat.' Harold Thimble was given to derogatory references to Chummy. Chummys at this point in time—he would say—are no longer content to feed decently on scraps, but daily devour out of tins stinking stuff equivalent in cost to quite a number of cigarettes.

'I don't know what you're on about, Harold.'

'I'm on about this thing of Dad's. Believing something's happening all over again. Of course it isn't. It's really happening for the first time *now*. Only it has slipped unnoticed past this first screen—consciousness, we've called it, haven't we?—and gone straight into the lumber-room. And then bounced back like.'

'Bounced back, Harold?'

'But not before it's collected a bit of dust, you might say. There it is, arrived in your consciousness all right, but wrapped in a whiff of the past. Which is why you kid yourself it has also happened before. That's *déjà vu*.'

'That's *what*, Harold?'

'*Déjà vu* is scientific.' Harold gave his explanation not without a hint of condescension. 'It's from this Latin, and means "seen already".'

Mrs Thimble, although she hadn't quite followed her son's exposition, was impressed by his learning. When she spoke again it was to say 'I see' in almost a humble fashion. But at this point, rather surprisingly, Samantha broke into the discussion sharply.

'But, Harold,' she said, 'you haven't heard the whole thing. There was that about the dirty photo, and about Albion Rovers, and about me and Chummy. But then he said, "Now there's going to be a terrible crash".'

'So what, kid?'

'When he said that about the crash, Harold, what he knew was going to happen—to happen *again*, he meant—hadn't happened *at all*. Or it hadn't unless I'm quite barmy, and Mum too. "Now there's going to be a terrible crash," he said. And almost directly after that, the big bang came. So it's a different thing, isn't it? There hadn't been anything to slip by into your lumber-room, and then bounce back all dusty-like into the front of his head.'

'It's a special case.' Harold's confidence had discernibly faltered, but he recovered himself at once. 'Dad was having this ordinary piece of *déjà vu*, like sometimes comes to everyone——'

'It hasn't to me,' Mrs Thimble said with some asperity. 'There's no such carryings on in *my* head, Harold.'

'You won't ever have noticed, Mum—not being an introspective type. But that's not the point. The point is that Dad was having this ordinary spot of *déjà vu*, when suddenly on top of it came a jab of precognitive experience.'

'Of *what*?'

'Precognitive experience. Suddenly seeing a bit of the future.'

'Like it might be Samantha's horoscopes, or your Auntie Flo's tea-leaves?'

'That's all just superstition, Mum. Precognitive experience is science. Only I wouldn't say science has got it quite taped yet. It's a sight less common than your old *déjà vu*. They go hunting for it in universities and places.' Harold's eyes suddenly lit up. 'Jesus!' he said. 'There might be something in it for Dad.'

'Something in it, Harold?'

'In a newspaper, say. With a photo of the two of you, Mum. And it could be built up like.' Harold's enthusiasm mounted. 'Front page stuff! "My life with a time-traveller." Thousands of pounds in it, there might be.'

'Harold Thimble, this is a respectable family that doesn't get itself in the papers, whether with photos or not. Precollywobbles and what have you! What next, I ask? I'll thank you to get on your feet and open a tin for Chummy.'

'Bloody cat,' Harold said. He had sprung to his feet, but was making for the door. 'There'll be reporters out there still, and I'm going after them. It'll be in the later editions in the morning. You'll see.'

And it was—although not with quite the prominence that Harold Thimble would have liked. There had, after all, been that torso up among the chimney pots, and several less drastically unfortunate persons were in hospital, so the early reports had to be given a sombre cast. 'Horror' and 'holocaust' attracted a good deal of large type, and there was a useful woman who had said, 'I was bathing the baby'. But one enterprising young reporter had got 'Plumstead Plumber's Premonition' past his sub-editors (plumbing being the elder Thimble's professional activity) and had fixed up an interview with the whole family for the following day. To this Mr Thimble was at first reluctant to agree. He wouldn't—he insisted with reasonable conviction—know what to say. And, anyway, what was there in it for him? Would the paper run to a tenner? For less than a fiver he just wouldn't do it. And that was flat.

With this unpromising simplicity of mind Harold had only a few hours in which to deal, and the result was undeniably a credit to him. He not only got his father to do as he was told on the spot, but also got into his head at least the rudiments of larger things to come. Albert Thimble just had to remember enough. The business of the big bang hadn't—had it?—been any mere flash in the pan. It only happened to be the most spectacular instance of a strange power that he had always known himself to possess. Even as a kid, Harold insisted. Wasn't that right?

Albert supposed that, yes, it was. He was doubtful about it at first, and even cast a mistrustful eye on his insistent son. But soon he was remembering one funny thing, and then another. These were muzzy convictions, and at first he knew them to be so. But he had always been secretly in awe of Harold's intellectual endowments, and even believed that it was mysteriously on account of them that the boy found it difficult to hold down a job. For years Harold must have been noting and remembering small but significant instances of those hitches in the temporal flow of things which he himself had forgotten about. And now Harold was saying there was money in it—and money very remote from the world of fivers and tenners and small jobs on drains and taps conducted on a cash-on-the-nail moonlighting basis. At first Harold didn't emphasize this aspect of the matter in any alarming way. But as his father softened up (for that is the expression we must use) he leant on it more heavily. So when the interview—the first interview—took place it didn't go too badly. There was even a photographer present, who for some reason took pictures of Samantha fondling Chummy. In this there may have been a designed suggestion that Samantha partook in some way of her father's supernormal powers. Witches go in for cats. When the young reporter did rather more poking about Mrs Thimble's kitchen than was quite polite, it may well have been in the hope of coming on a broomstick.

It was Mrs Thimble who was a bit of a snag. 'Respectable' remained her key word. They'd always been respectable in Number 14, and this just wasn't. She would have liked to say that it was all nonsense too. But this she found she couldn't do. She was at bottom a clear-headed woman, and if the fact didn't often appear it may have been because she had frequently found the endowment disadvantageous in domestic situations. She very much disliked the brouhaha being created by Harold and acquiesced in by his father. But she didn't lose sight of the fact that something very strange had really happened in Number 14 when there had been that nasty incident in Number 36.

Quite a batch of articles was concocted about the Plumstead plumber's second sight. As these soon included what purported to be reminiscences not only on his own part but on the part of his children as well, a lot of money came in—although it was not, indeed, quite on the scale hopefully anticipated by Harold. And, of course, the affair lasted no time at all. Even so, it allowed for what was to be the fateful interposition of Dr Cudbird.

Dr Cudbird was a reader in Parapsychology, and had been given his job by a sceptical university as being himself the most comprehensively sceptical of the people who had put in for it. But he was a conscientious man, open to weighing even anecdotal material, and not averse to field-work. When a piece of nonsense turned up even in the most vulgar of the public prints he went and had a look at it. Or if he didn't go himself he sent Kidder, a young man—perhaps unfortunately named in the circumstances—who was called an Assistant Lecturer, and who constituted under his chief the entire strength of the Department of Psychical Research. (The old lady who put up the money had insisted on 'Psychical Research', the word 'parapsychology' not having been invented when she had begun to interest herself in poltergeists and table-turnings.)

'You've been keeping an eye on those Thimbles?' Cudbird asked his junior colleague. 'They're still actively on the map. The latest is their having an unaccountable cat. "The Case of the Unaccountable Cat". It sounds like the title of an old-fashioned detective story.'

'I'm afraid I'm not up with the cat.'

'It has only just entered the *dramatis personae*. Name of

Chummy. It sees things in corners. More commonly that's dogs.'

'So it is.'

'At least they haven't yet disembowelled the creature and consulted the entrails. Haruspication may pass current in the Edgware Road, but it hasn't reached Plumstead.' Dr Cudbird paused on this, but Kidder gave no sign of having recognized an elegant reference to the muse of T.S. Eliot. 'Those Thimbles are clearly out to squeeze their lemon till the pips squeak,' Cudbird continued on a more colloquial note. 'Go and have a look, before they drop out of sight.'

'Would there be much point in it?' Initially, at least, Kidder saw no satisfaction as likely to result from a pilgrimage to Pipkin Grove. 'It's clear that a lot of hocus-pocus——'

'Yes, of course,' Cudbird interrupted impatiently. 'But it's our business to show that we do investigate. And investigation ought not to stop short in face of an element of fraud or absurdity. There's always the argument that investigation itself tends to inhibit the play of genuinely paranormal forces, and that the psychical mediums and all their kidney tend then to take to cheating simply to keep their end up.'

'And the cash flowing in. Yes, I know.' Kidder was inclined to resent his chief's frequent enunciation of professional platitudes. 'But of course I'll make a recce if you want me to. After all, our own cash has to keep flowing in as well.' This was a reference to something uncomfortably probationary in the status of the Department of Parapsychology. There were persons powerful in the councils of the university who would happily have seen that dotty old lady's intentions unobtrusively betrayed, and her benefaction diverted to more orthodox academic activities. 'So I'll give those Thimbles a short, sharp go-over, and report back.'

And a few days later Kidder did report.

'There's this elderly couple,' he said. 'A plumber and his wife. Too thick to invent much, I'd say.'

'*Unusually* stupid?' The Reader in Parapsychology went in for brisk queries.

'They certainly wouldn't shine in any I.Q. test. Of course, they are in a bewildering situation. Thimble seems out of his depth and in a bit of a funk. There's a shade more sense in his wife. They're both insistent that the queer thing did happen. So is the daughter, an empty-headed girl who does hairdressing. The son, Harold Thimble, wasn't present in the old home when the explosion occurred, but he had plenty to say. Rather clever, Harold is—and with a bit of reading to him. Chattered about *déjà vu*. He even knew to call it a type of paramnesia.'

'You think that suspicious?'

'Well, it can be read as that. But since the thing happened——'

'If it did.'

'Quite so. I was going to say he'd quite naturally have been taking a dekko at the textbooks and little dictionaries. Harold's out of work. He may be a public library type. But he didn't know the term "concatenate paramnesia".'

'As it occurs only in an obscure paper of your own, Kidder, that is not markedly to the young man's discredit.'

'The phenomenon's obscure, too. But it certainly exists. Several *déjà-vu* impressions come huddled rapidly one after the other. And—just occasionally—there immediately follows what I call the converse persuasion. One switches from thinking "This has happened before . . . and now this . . . and this" to thinking "And now here's what's *going* to happen".'

'And has it ever been certainly known to?'

'I rather think not. You see, it's very rare, very fugitive——'

'And totally insusceptible of experimental verification?'

'Well, naturally. But I'm convinced——'

'Just where was Harold Thimble when the explosion took place?'

'Cruising round on his motor-bike, he says.'

'And how had it affected his father?'

'Albert Thimble was naturally pretty upset, and he said he'd go out and get a breath of air. Actually, it's known he went round to a pub, and talked about the thing rather incoherently.'

'And he's done a good deal of talking since?'

'Certainly he has. To journalists, and much under his son's

eye. That element of fraud and absurdity has arrived, all right. If I ever write up this thing, I think I'll call it the phase of remunerative confabulation.'

'Very pretty, no doubt. But you're too fond of giving names to things, Kidder. Savages go for it, thinking they get power over the unaccountable that way. But it's delusive.'

'Thanks for the warning.' Kidder was nettled. 'I think I'd rather you went and made a further recce yourself.'

'In fact, you're rather impressed, but don't want to go out on a limb about it?'

'You can put it that way. It *might* just be important. Anything touching on the world-wide and aeons-old tradition of vaticination merits scrutiny by more than one investigator.'

'I rather agree with you there.'

'And either those two women are lying about what Albert Thimble said just then, or we've come upon a fairly positive piece of testimony. Isn't that undeniable?'

'No, it is not. In fact, Kidder, I must tell you that you haven't quite thought the thing through. Sleep on it further, my dear boy.' Cudbird, who knew perfectly well that he was being insulting, managed to give this advice with an appearance of the utmost benevolence and good feeling. 'And I'll certainly do as you ask, and go out to Plumstead. The road to Endor, eh?' And the Reader in Parapsychology laughed easily. He seemed actually to believe—Kidder told himself—that he had achieved a witticism.

At Number 14 Harold Thimble was coming to feel not quite easy in his mind. He believed that he had handled the reporters and 'feature writers' pretty well. Almost without exception, they had been easy game. For one thing, they hadn't armed themselves, as he had done, with a day or two's crash-course in psychical research. And for another, they weren't very distinguishably interested in the truth. Investigative journalists (which is what they called themselves) probably came to feel —almost without being conscious of the fact—that too much of the truth is apt to be awkwardly boring. Or so Harold, now so heavily committed to the proposition that fiction has the edge on truth every time, firmly believed.

It had been different with Kidder, the young man from college, who was apparently some sort of professor's mate or hodman. Kidder seemed to believe that truth was what was left in the sieve after you'd done a great deal of vigorous riddling, and that it was the part of the package you ought to be interested in. He'd been quite unprepared to buy the notion that Number 14 was a house at which all sorts of unaccountable happenings were lavishly on offer. And yet there *were* such houses. The books said so. There were the ones, for instance, in which harmless objects kept on tumbling off shelves or even hurtling across the room. Nor had Kidder been interested in Chummy, who could make a mutton bone behave in this satisfactory fashion simply by fixing her eye on it and mewing thrice. Actually, Harold rather regretted the play of his own inventive mind on Chummy, even although 'Do Cats Have Nine Senses?' had made a distinctly arresting headline. The business about Chummy seeing things you didn't see, and being unspeakably terrified as a result, had even brought a man from the Cruelty to Animals, who was quite cross when he found nothing but an obviously contented and well-nourished pet.

And Samantha was a bother. Samantha was perfectly willing to go along with her brother's racket so long as there was something in it for her. But by this she didn't only mean cash. She wanted a role as well. And it had to be a romantic role. Having come across the expression heaven knew where, she had settled for a Demon Lover. Her nightly struggles to maintain her maiden condition against the advances of this monster (Robot-like, and lit up from inside as by electricity) would no doubt have made good salacious reading. But Harold had to veto them. They mustn't, he said, report anything too extravagant.

But there was a further worry. The Gas Board had, of course, announced the instituting of an immediate inquiry into the disaster at Number 36. But rather a long time had now gone by without any announcement or finding in the matter. This ought not to have affected the Thimbles at all. No Thimble had been an eye-witness, let alone an agent, in the affair, and Albert Thimble's strange experience, even when vigorously hyped by the joint efforts of his son and the metropolitan press, was none of the Gas Board's business. Yet the Board had twice sent a nosy fellow along to Number 14, and on the second occasion he was accompanied by a little man who would have been totally undistinguished had he not possessed an intent gaze through a pair of unnaturally pale-blue and glittering eyes. Harold hadn't a doubt that he belonged to the fuzz. And although Harold's conscience was clear (or the next thing to it) he found this distinctly disturbing.

Finally, there was Dad. Albert, although a good deal in awe of the bright speed of his son's mind, wasn't at all easy about his own sudden fame. He doubted, he said, whether it was at all good for plumbing. His clientele lay in the main within an unassuming stratum of society, and got the world's news either from the box or from the kind of newspaper that Harold had so successfully cultivated. People mightn't greatly fancy having around the house a plumber who perhaps had advance information of what was going to happen to them next week. The Leather Bottle was difficult, too. It chanced to enjoy considerable custom from the local betting fraternity. These people, whether in chaff or because of an honest persuasion of having an oracle in their midst, were inclined to badger Albert about the winner of the next day's 2.30 at Cheltenham.

Reviewing these domestic circumstances and the situation in general, Harold felt that the time had come to draw in, as it were, his ectoplasmic horns; to wind up the brief but remunerative history of Number 14 as a kind of fun-fair palace of extra-sensory perception. Most of the money from the papers he had managed to keep under his own hand, and it seemed to be enough to start a modest business on. Uncle Ned had probably made do with less. There were risks, of course, but there were chances as well. Youth Redeployment was risk-free—or risk-free if you discounted the possibility of being run over by a bus on the way to it. But on the scale of chances it seemed to Harold to register an absolute zero, whereas a discreet little video 'library' or 'club' might do very nicely. He had been out one evening in pursuit of this artistic venture when, on getting home, he found his family with a visitor he didn't much like the look of. Another rozzer, he said to himself at once, like the nasty little man with the pale-blue eyes. Then he saw this wasn't quite right. Here was just one more journalist, although not quite like those with whom he had recently (and profitably) become familiar. What they called the 'quality' press had probably sent this rather senior person. But such persons—supercilious, they'd be—were (to put it mildly) out of place in Pipkin Grove. So Harold decided to begin on the winding-up phase of things pretty vigorously here and now.

'My parents doing the polite, are they?' he asked the visitor. 'Well, I'll tell you something. Enough's enough, see? We've *had* the bloody media, and you'll oblige us by fucking off.'

'Really now, Harold!' Mrs Thimble said.

'Dad here has this strange experience, with Mum and Samantha witnesses to it, don't forget. And we done our best to satisfy legitimate public curiosity like. But since then our house has had a load of bloody nonsense tipped over it by you and your mob from the papers.' Harold paused for a moment, perhaps to admire this small exculpatory exercise. Then he rose to more elevated considerations. 'The claims of science, now: a responsible citizen has to meet them. But he needn't lend himself to cheap sensation. So just sod off, chum, and do us a favour. Get where you can nose around a bit for a spot of bondage and rape.'

'But Harold, dear, the gentleman *is* science!' This came from Mrs Thimble in a kind of wail, and certainly without any consciousness of achieving a trope of rhetoric.

'*Are* you?' Harold demanded.

'Yes, I am.' Dr Cudbird (for of course the visitor was he) spoke testily and perhaps without quite considering what he was assenting to. And in one regard, indeed, he was not at the moment personifying science at all well. Instinctively and without having any cool thought to the matter, he was disliking this intolerable young man very much—and he didn't much care for the young man's father, either. Moreover, he was rather at a loss how, if at all, to proceed. 'And my name,' he managed to add, 'is Cudbird'.

There was no reaction to this—nor would there have been, in all probability, had he said, 'My name is Ozymandias' or 'My name is Might-have-been' or something similar out of poetry. The young man simply scowled, and took a species of token kick at the Thimble family cat—which had been dozing on the hearthrug without evincing any disposition to see things mere humans didn't see. But then the elder Mr Thimble spoke.

'Take it easy, son,' he said. 'It's right enough the gent isn't from the papers. He's the same as that Kipper was here a matter of days ago. Sent by Kipper, like as not.'

'Kidder,' Dr Cudbird said with dignity. 'And Mr Kidder is my Research Assistant.'

'There!' Albert Thimble said. 'So you see, son. No word on cash down yet. But it's not like the papers, with a rush job and a deadline right ahead of them. That'll come—see?' The elder Thimble lowered his voice a shade—apparently under the grotesque persuasion that this would render him inaudible to the visitor. 'And just be civil, Harold. Don't get putting the gent's back up. Not prudent, it wouldn't be. Not after the way we've worked it.'

The elder Mr Thimble's was clearly not a very lucid mind. There might be much behind this last remark, or there might be almost nothing at all. But it evidently hinted at that element of fraud or absurdity in spite of which—as Cudbird had insisted to his young colleague—psychic research must press on unregarding. Cudbird, however, quite failed to press on now. Prior to Harold Thimble's arriving home, he had got very little out of Harold's parents—and out of Samantha Thimble (who appeared to be much attracted to light periodical literature), he had got precisely as much as out of Chummy the unaccountable cat. So that if he left Number 14 forthwith, it would be with a nil score so far as parapsychology was concerned. Nevertheless, he got to his feet without hesitation.

'I must go away at once,' he said. 'I have no warrant whatsoever to impose myself on you. I must therefore——'

'Warrant!' Albert Thimble interrupted—plainly as much in alarm as bewilderment.

' . . . say good-afternoon,' Cudbird concluded—and he even managed to make the elder Thimbles a kind of formal bow. Harold Thimble, whose language had been so outrageous, he decided to ignore; and as for Samantha, Samantha ignored *him*. But the order of his going was unimportant. In this wretched little plebeian dwelling he wasn't merely in the presence of fraud; he was in the presence of fraud and nothing else whatever. Professionally, there was no scrap of evidence upon which to pause. Socially, the occasion had been decidedly not a success. He was glad to leave the dust of Pipkin Grove behind him.

But—metaphorically, at least—the dust was not so easily shaken off. It turned up in Cudbird's Department a couple of days later in the form of a plain-clothes policeman—and with so little ceremony that it actually interrupted the Department's two members endeavouring to make sense of a discouraging mass of statistics unloaded on them by a much larger kindred concern in North Carolina. The policeman (who had piercing light-blue eyes) was, however, properly polite.

'My name's Gibson,' he said. 'I'm troubling you, gentlemen, because I understand you've both had some concern with this haunted house.'

'This haunted house?' Cudbird repeated sternly. (Cudbird detested haunted houses.)

'In Plumstead, sir.'

'Ah, our friends the Thimbles,' Kidder said. Kidder had what Cudbird considered to be a somewhat insubordinate habit of chipping in. 'But I'm not clear about the haunting, Mr Gibson. Do you regard Chummy Thimble as a reliable witness?'

'*Chummy* Thimble, sir?'

'The cat. Chummy Thimble is the Thimble cat. And only Chummy suggests herself as seeing ghosts. Or such is my impression. But undeniably the family Thimble has been going in for miscellaneous supernatural high-jinks for quite some time now.'

'Exactly, sir—and harmless-enough nonsense most of it seems to have been. But there's been money in it, and the question arises as to whether it has been gained by false pretences.' With an air of some consequence, Gibson produced a notebook. 'Hence these inquiries.'

'Quite right,' Cudbird said.

'Quite wrong,' Kidder said, promptly and cheerfully. 'You wouldn't get any support from the papers that paid for the stuff, since their own journalists must have had a hand in most of it. But I suspect, Inspector, that you're really after something else. The big bang it all started from, isn't it?'

'Well, yes, Mr Kidder. We're not happy about that explosion.'

'By which you mean,' Cudbird asked sharply, 'the fact, or the assertion, that the elder Thimble knew when it was about to happen?'

'Fair enough, Professor.' (Gibson clearly felt this to be a judicious form of address.) 'If something criminal was supected as being involved, and the whole affair came to court, handling that stuff about precognition—I gather it's called that—might be uncommonly tricky. I'd like to feel, myself, that we had one or two expert witnesses to call upon.'

'I see.' It was clear that what Dr Cudbird saw was far from pleasing him. 'I doubt whether on further thought, Mr Gibson, you will view the matter quite in that light. It is a matter, incidentally, on which I can recall recommending further thought to Mr Kidder here.'

'Or further sleep,' Kidder said. 'I was instructed to sleep on it. Quite rightly.'

'In fact,' Cudbird said, 'there was nothing precognitive, or parapsychic, or super-what-have-you involved at all. Fraud from start to finish.'

'So Mrs Thimble and her daughter were both lying about the man's having said, "Now there's going to be an explosion", or whatever it was?'

'That's where I went wrong,' Kidder said—again cheerfully. 'Asking that one. The women *may* have been lying—in which case they are part of a criminal conspiracy—or they may not. At the moment, we can take our choice. Right, Cudbird?'

'Essentially, yes.' Cudbird appeared to feel that his junior colleague was conducting his part in this discussion with an inappropriate lightness of air. 'The way I see the matter, Inspector, is this. Harold Thimble—to my mind, a most objectionable young man—is idle and unemployed. He is also clever, and with a smattering of knowledge in one field or another. I seem to recall some poet as remarking that a little knowledge is a dangerous thing.'

'Alexander Pope,' Kidder explained to Gibson—and added, 'Dr Cudbird, you notice, has a smattering of literature.'

'Harold Thimble'—Cudbird ignored this cheap gibe—'evolves a scheme for making a little money out of the popular papers. Something striking must be made to occur in the neighbourhood, and his father is to be represented as the possessor of an abnormal power which gives him prior notice of whatever it may be. That was the general idea.' Dr Cudbird paused on this. 'It must be understood, Inspector,' he added impressively, 'that at this point I am merely forming a hypothesis.'

'Which can be tested by experiment?' Kidder asked swiftly.

'My dear young man, we are not in that kind of situation. What we may perhaps hope for is confession.'

'With the Inspector, here, getting out the thumb-screws and giving the rack a thorough dust down? Cudbird, go on.'

'Very well. Let us suppose that Mrs Thimble and her daughter have been telling the truth. It's my own impression, for what it's worth, that they have, in fact, been doing so.'

'If we're to have impressions on the table,' Kidder said, 'mine's the same. The wenches just haven't got successful lying in them—or not in the face of reasonable interrogation. Inspector, you must have something to say about that. They're too thick, aren't they?'

'I wouldn't say it was quite that.' Gibson shook a misdoubting head. 'I've known very low intelligence go along with successful deception often enough—and under skilled professional questioning, mark you. But I'm bound to say my own impression is the same as yours and Dr Cudbird's, sir. At least about that first stage of the affair, the women are telling the truth. Thimble made that remark, and the explosion followed.'

'Very well,' Cudbird said. 'We have a plot incubated by Harold, and with only his father in the know. Just what is required before, so to speak, he can hatch it? Just two things, it seems to me. The first is the ability to cause an explosion in the neighbourhood. A moderate sort of explosion is no doubt what he aimed at: not the horrific affair he eventually achieved. No great difficulty in contriving *that*. The second thing he required was accurate timing. And what was needed *there*? I think I can tell you, Inspector.' Dr Cudbird, although a distinguished scientist, was not above a little dramatic effect, so here he made a short pause. 'A couple of watches, reasonably synchronized.'

'And that's it!' Springing to his feet and glancing at his own watch, Detective-Inspector Gibson might have been calculating just how quickly he could find a magistrate and secure a warrant. 'Simple fraud from start to finish!'

'Nothing but that,' Dr Cudbird said. 'Nothing at all.'

So Albert Thimble and his son were arrested (or it looked like that) with ignominious publicity—being hustled into a police car while the neighbours gaped, and Mrs Thimble and her daughter wept, and plucky little Chummy Thimble hissed in impotent fury. It was, of course, a serious affair—for had not half of an unoffending citizen ended on a chimney-stack? But although a charge of manslaughter lay with some certainty ahead, Albert and Harold found upon arrival at a police station that they were merely helping the constabulary with their inquiries into the late affair at Number 36 Pipkin Grove. In the following morning's papers they had become simply 'two men'. 'Two men' etc were helping the police etc. . . . It was like that, and could so continue to be for some days without legal complications. Few countries are more obviously than England a home of the free.

But then, on the third day, Dr Cudbird was called to the telephone.

'Gibson here. Your synchronized watches, sir. They won't wash.'

'Won't wash?' Momentarily, Dr Cudbird was so at sea that he found himself reflecting that one doesn't send watches, whether synchronized or not, to the laundry. 'Just what do you mean, Inspector?'

'I mean that those two Thimbles—and pretty rascals they are—have ceased to help us with our inquiries. They've gone home. In a taxi, so as not to attract notice. Only somebody split on us, and there were photographers waiting. Curse that damned Gas Board.'

'Inspector Gibson, you forget yourself. But explain.'

'They've come out with their report, after the very devil of a delay. They've had to dig deep, they say. Literally that. They've found a fractured main in a deep conduit. The stuff wandered about underground, and then chose to snug up in that accursed Number 36. And the whole thing, of course, utterly beyond young Harold Thimble's contriving. You might as well accuse him of having sunk a bloody battleship.'

'I see.'

'As for the start of it all, sir, you may feel it deserves thought.'

'Quite so.' Dr Cudbird paused, and found that no further words occurred to him. 'Quite so,' he repeated, and rang off.

MELENCOLIA I

I

Charles Bibury, although possessing rather more of general information than most prosperous and busy painters bother to pick up, had never heard of Ambrose Scurl. So when the woman sitting next to him evidently thought to clinch her proposal by saying quietly, 'My father is Ambrose Scurl', Bibury had to decide whether to look frankly and regretfully blank, or to pretend to knowledge he didn't possess and hope for the best.

'Yes, indeed,' he said. 'Your very kind suggestion attracts me strongly, I need hardly say. But, just at present, there are rather formidable difficulties. In fact, insuperable ones, I'm sorry to have to confess.'

In introducing him to the woman while marshalling her guests, his hostess had named her as Mrs Blond, and they'd hardly sat down before Mrs Blond explained that she was now a widow, and 'kept house' for her father, who was 'wonderful for his years'. This was a shade more rapidly communicative in the personal way than Bibury regarded as appropriate in dinner-party chat. So he had decided that Mrs Blond was a bit of a bore, and through the soup and fish he talked for the most part with the woman on his other hand, a lively old soul he'd known for many years. But then Mrs Blond had come back at him to an even odder effect. Would he consider, she wanted to know, accepting a commission to paint her father's portrait? Bibury was startled. With a young and almost unknown artist the abruptness of the thing would have been pardonable and probably agreeable. To come thus head-on at a person of his eminence (and eminent he was obliged to know that he was, whether deservedly or not) wasn't at all in order. But he mustn't, of course, snub a fellow guest, so what seemed to be needed was a rather elaborate courtesy. It was when he embarked on this that Mrs Blond interrupted with the information that her father was Ambrose Scurl.

Bibury persevered with polite explanations. He didn't say that he was accustomed to receive all such overtures through an agent, and still less that his London agent had confirmed with an opposite number in New York that a specified acreage of carefully applied pigment should be available for exhibition in six months' time. But he did say roundly that over a long period ahead he had promised more than he feared he might be able to perform. Otherwise, of course. . . .

'And a replica,' Mrs Blond said, disregarding. 'There would have to be a replica. We have to think, you see, of the National Portrait Gallery.'

'Gracious lady, I *never* paint replicas. No doubt there is respectable precedent for such things in the history of painting—and even of sculpture—since the *cinquecento*. But it seems to me unnatural and uncreative, and I've never gone in for it. Copies are another matter. The legal position about them is, I am told, obscure. But I'd never object to the taking of one. Indeed, I've found a reliable man, a copyist whom I use from time to time.' Bibury paused on this. 'Or a reliable lady,' he added.

'I will write to you,' Mrs Blond said with surprising dignity. 'Have you been to Glyndebourne lately?'

On the following evening Bibury, a bachelor with old-fashioned habits, dined alone in his club. But afterwards he ran into a man called Micklethwaite, who was some sort of don at Oxford. They drank a glass of port together.

'Micklethwaite,' it occurred to Bibury to ask, 'did you ever hear of somebody called Ambrose Scurl?'

'Well, yes.' Micklethwaite, who owned the somewhat unpolished manners frequently to be remarked in the academic world, allowed himself to look surprised. 'The philosopher, of course.'

'And at the top of his tree?' This was always a point of some importance with Charles Bibury.

'*Quondam* very much so, I'd say. But outmoded now. A very glum philosopher. Only on the foundations of unyielding despair can the temple of the human spirit henceforth. . . .'

'This Scurl talked like that?'

'That I can't say, never having heard him converse. But he certainly wrote in some such fashion.'

'But *is* that kind of feel about things wholly outmoded? I'd have thought that with the general existentialist persuasion that we've been plonked down in a set-up that's totally absurd. . . .'

'That's rather different.' Micklethwaite's tone hinted indulgence, so that it occurred to Bibury that the man was probably a philosopher himself, and not a devotee of numismatics, papyrology, or what-have-you in the learned Oxford way. 'I suppose you're thinking of Sartre and his crowd,' Micklethwaite went on. 'One has to remember that they evolved their philosophy during the German occupation of France, when being passive just wasn't on among decent chaps. So they made a good deal of the plain fact that every man can choose to act one way or the other. Whether or not Scurl came to pay any attention to them, I don't know. He belongs essentially to an earlier time. Pretty well to Nietzsche, in fact, and the death of God.'

'Ah, yes—the death of God.' Bibury hastened to show that he was *au fait* with this interesting historical event. Then he produced what he judged to be a reasonably well-informed question. 'Schopenhauer, now: would he come into this Scurl's picture?'

'I'd suppose so. At least they can both be called pessimists. Most philosophers are optimists, after a fashion.'

Bibury now felt that this talk was in some danger of turning into what Micklethwaite would term a tutorial, and that he ought to shift to his own ground.

'Optimism and pessimism are a bit off my beat,' he said. 'But it's otherwise with success and failure—and I see irritatingly more of one than the other. Modern portraiture has become an adjunct of the success story. Some inane society woman is brought into my studio, and I have to make it apparent for all to see that she gave the most triumphant ball of the season. Or I try to cope with some red-faced, over-dieted fellow who would have it known on the canvas that he has just brought off a tremendous killing in the City. I believe "killing" is the word.'

'I understand that it must be taxing. Yet think, Bibury, of those of your *confrères* who are perpetually painting horses. Having to impart an impression of conscious worth to a Derby winner must be yet more boring—and demeaning, if you like. I've sometimes suspected, incidentally, that losing horses are conscious of defeat while winning ones are unaware of having distinguished themselves. If that's so, the painter is required positively to cheat, is he not? And it's hard cheese on the horses.' Micklethwaite paused, apparently to admire his involved whimsy. 'Why are you curious about Scurl?'

'It's only a passing curiosity. I've been asked to take on painting his portrait, but it's out of the question. I'm full up for a long way ahead.'

'With red-faced and over-dieted tycoons? Scurl would be something of a change from that. If you have an itch to ditch success and go slumming after failure, he might prove just your man.'

Bibury didn't judge this consideration to have been expressed with much amenity, and he took his leave of Micklethwaite as soon as he had finished his port. But as he retrieved his hat and coat from the chilly and marble-clad recesses of the club he had to acknowledge having received something to think about. *He* was successful, and thought of himself as by temperament well-equipped to enjoy success. Yet success lurkingly irked him through a feeling that he had come by it on the cheap; failure such as this fellow Scurl's drew him because, at least by the ultimate standards, he was a failure himself. He hadn't even (he concluded with an unaccustomed dip into morbidity) the honesty to *look* a failure. If he set up an affair of mirrors and went about a self-portrait what emerged on the canvas would be something red-faced and over-dieted.

These thoughts absorbed him for some time, so that when he suddenly laughed aloud he was disconcerted to find that for this unseemly demonstration he had come to a halt in a public street, garish with neon lighting, smelly with petrol fumes. He walked on hastily, but his thoughts kept pace with him. Sometimes he still envisaged a miracle: the coming to him from some mysterious beyond of what the scribbling art historians called a third manner. It was the most idle of notions. A third manner comes only to a tiny minority even of those artists who have authentically achieved a first manner and then a second one, and in that whole league he simply didn't play. In what might be called a high-class academic fashion, he was frankly a commercial artist. It was as simple as that, and he lived with it perfectly comfortably for most of the time. Yes, here he was, a busy little chap scurrying towards a London bus stop, dreaming of Donatello, of Michelangelo and *terribilità*! Pitiful, he told himself cheerfully, pitiful. And what had started off this useless reverie? A conjectural image of the unknown Ambrose Scurl, failed or outmoded philosopher, as having with dignity come to terms with his own condition, living in retirement, resolved at least to make himself no motley to the view. The real Scurl was probably quite different: embittered and fidgety; insisting he had been unfairly treated in *Mind* in 1940; intent on getting himself at life-size and half-length into their blessed National Portrait Gallery. His daughter's assault tended to bear out at least this last assumption. A most insistent woman.

The insistent woman's letter was on his breakfast-table next morning. Bibury was rather struck by it. Without ceasing to be business-like it did briefly touch on a point of sentiment. Her father was in his eighty-first year; his tenure of life had to be thought about; she possessed a few mediocre photographs of him; and death-masks were—were they not?—happily outmoded. She then named a fee that doubled Bibury's going rate even when extorted from livery companies or multinational conglomerates. Initially, Bibury discounted this last consideration. Mrs Blond would have second thoughts about her cheque as soon as she started inquiring around. But then it came to Bibury—just as a matter of curiosity—to consult reference books. The woman's deceased husband turned out to have been a tax-haven type of the first order. His initial million had been in his pocket almost before his pockets were in long trousers, and he hadn't looked back thereafter. It perhaps said something for his widow that with the world's playfields presumably at her command she had fixed herself up housekeeping for her father, an obscure cough-in-ink philosopher. Mrs Blond concluded her letter with a touch of grandeur somewhat alien, however, to the mores of the professional classes. She named an hour in the day at which she was accustomed to be at home.

Bibury succumbed—not with any intention of taking the job, since his time-table was not to be tinkered with for at least some months ahead. It was simply that he felt curious about Ambrose Scurl. He could take a look at the old boy, and even perhaps have some talk with him, during a call that could easily be represented as a necessary courtesy to his daughter. He'd enter a little more fully into the circumstances forbidding him to undertake what would have been a most interesting commission, and come away with a small accession to his knowledge of human nature in senescence.

Such was at least his conscious view of his behaviour as a taxi took him up to Hampstead. The senescence to be inspected proved to harbour in a large but commonplace house with the Heath and its ponds conveniently at the back door. Bibury wondered whether the aged philosopher took a daily toddle there, observing the flying kites and the small boys angling for suppositious fish; perhaps, like the poet Swinburne at Putney, pausing to pat the heads of infants in their well-sprung perambulators. Swinburne had been provided with a fixed sum of money in order to recruit himself with a moderate draught of sherry for the return to his guardian at The Pines. Would Scurl, Bibury wondered, prove to have passed under a similar suzerainty at the hands of his devoted daughter? Would he, for instance, so much as have heard of any project for the painting of his portrait—let alone himself be whoring after so shadowy an immortality as might be conferred by that compendious receptacle off Trafalgar Square? It was an amusing question which must presently resolve itself.

He rang a bell. The door was opened—as, just occasionally, doors were still opened for Bibury—by a manservant. His inquiry was received in silence but with an acquiescent bow; he was led through a shadowy hall; a further door was opened before him.

'Sir Charles Bibury!' the man announced—as loudly as if into the din of a large reception, but in some indescribable fashion rather mournfully as well.

Bibury's eyes ought to have been immediately upon his hostess, who had risen to greet him, but for perceptible moments they were on the walls of the room. The girl getting out of the bath was Renoir, the bridge spanning the water-lily pond was Monet's bridge at Giverny, Mont St Victoire beneath an archway of pine boughs was Cézanne. There was a Seurat, a Gauguin, a Van Gogh. It might have been called rather a 'safe' collection, but such a prodigality of Impressionism and Post-Impressionism in private hands surprised Bibury a good deal. He wondered whether the display had been brought together by the lady now before him or by her deceased husband the tycoon. Or was it conceivable that Ambrose Scurl himself was a man of taste, and had masterminded an operation which his daughter's opulence made feasible? One obvious question presented itself at once. With all this interest in art around, why had it taken these people so long to get busy about a portrait of the philosophic Scurl? They could have had their pick of a succession of swells. They could have had the ageing John. They could have gone out on a limb a little and had Sutherland. They could have gone a good deal further out and had Kokoschka. Instead of which there was this belated proposal. So Bibury would have to stand in the middle of all these monstrously valuable canvases and reiterate that he himself had no time for daddy Ambrose. Altogether it was an awkward business. He wished he hadn't come.

'Sir Charles, how kind of you to call.'

The woman was doing her stuff. Presently there would be a tinkle of teacups and a plate of macaroons. But would there be a philosopher? Perhaps Scurl was bedridden. At his age that would be fair enough. Conceivably it was envisaged that their chosen artist should get to work not on a sitter but a permanently supine person: Scurl *in articulo mortis*. Wasn't there some poet or other who'd had himself painted in his shroud? Bibury had a brief vision of trying to cope with a dying man's fingers as they plucked and plucked feebly at some sheet or coverlet. At least, he told himself, you can't be expected to paint a death-rattle. They'd have to import some sort of electronic gadget if they wanted to commemorate that.

This macabre line of thought was dispelled first by Mrs Blond's devoting a few minutes to small talk and then by the predicted appearance of the tea things. 'Tea equipage' would perhaps have been the more fitting term, since what was paraded ran to a little blue flame, a good deal of silver, and what Bibury rather nervously took to be Sèvres. Mrs Blond, however, performed briskly rather than with any considered elegance before all this paraphernalia.

'My father,' she said, 'will join us in a few minutes. It is his habit to take a glass of brandy and soda at this hour. But he has a fancy for making rather a private business of it.'

So here was another possible view of the situation. Dreary old Ambrose was a drunk of long standing. Ever so long ago, feeling his power to philosophize slipping away from him, he'd taken to sitting too often and too long over the decanters in some drab college common-room. Now they'd succeeded in hauling the inebriate sage at least half on to the water wagon. He needed a tot or two before facing up to company, but it was judged that he was at last presentable even for the acid test of portraiture.

'I much look forward to meeting the professor,' Bibury said formally. (That Scurl was, or had been, a professor seemed a safe enough bet.) 'But I'm terribly afraid that I'm taking up his and your time most unwarrantably. I've really only come to repeat that, most unhappily . . .'

At this moment the door opened and Ambrose Scurl came into the room. He was above the middle height, and he was in a deep depression. These two disparate facts were simultaneously apparent. Scurl didn't have to speak, he didn't even have to give you a look, before his nervous condition revealed itself. Here was no philosopher a little daunted by the eternal silence of the heavens, or even by the discovery that we share our planet with eleven-foot submarine tube-worms endowed with the capacity to absorb nourishing bacteria through their skin. Here was simply something which, if unsheltered by wealth and position, would subsist in a bin huddled with others of its kind in a drug-conditioned muted misery. And what made this so instantly manifest was the man's moving within an aura of isolation, of detachment, which one seemed, paradoxically, to *hear* as a kind of unnatural soundlessness which for the moment was more commanding than anything one clearly *saw* about him. That Mrs Blond, with such a parent on her hands, should nourish the project she did seemed to Charles Bibury an unbearable folly.

Scurl advanced and shook hands with his visitor. He produced a polite murmur without, one felt, himself hearing it. He picked up an old-fashioned three-tier cake stand and elevated it in air so that Bibury could inspect, and choose from, a plate of *petits fours*. Then he sat down with an appearance of faint expectation, as if aware that conversation was something that sometimes happened and was possibly going forward in his daughter's drawing-room now. Bibury was impressed by these evidences of good-breeding inflexibly maintained amid adverse circumstances. But he was a painter, and what compelled him more powerfully was the physical man. Scurl was spare rather than emaciated, but with cheek-bones so pronounced and thrusting as to seem about to break through their integument. They were also curiously slanted, so that if in fact projected as seemed to threaten they would act as a pair of pincers nipping the tip of the philosopher's nose. Yet—as if here were a sketch by Leonardo of some old man glimpsed in the street—this note of grotesque had its own dignity as somehow speaking of the spirit struggling through the clay. Quite suddenly, Bibury knew that a challenge confronted him. In the strict sense of the word, Ambrose Scurl was *pittoresco*. There was nothing for it. He'd have to paint the man.

Bibury had known such abrupt compulsions before, and believed they were not uncommon with artists generally. But in this case there was a hidden complexity of motivation. Scurl wasn't merely visually stimulating in a tantalizing way; he somehow at once occasioned one of Bibury's intermittent lapses from serenity, induced that lurking feeling that he hadn't got as far—or was it aimed as high?—as he might have done. He felt, in fact, a slightly frightening bond with the man! And Scurl was none of the things he had imagined, was not nobly and tranquilly resigned on the one hand, nor petty and embittered on the other. Had he been a fated depressive from his cradle, or was that just the way his missing out on high distinction had taken him? Here was perhaps a question for the consulting-room rather than the atelier. Nevertheless, Bibury felt it relevant to what must go on canvas.

The immediate problem was the awkwardness of contriving a plausible volte-face, since he had laid on rather thick to Mrs Blond the extent of his existing commitments over an indefinite period ahead. It was something to tackle boldly and at once. He set down his tea-cup.

'I need hardly repeat,' he said, 'that I'd very much like. . . .' But at once he had to come to an awkward pause. He had been about to address Mrs Blond and say, '. . . to paint your father's portrait'. Just in time, he had seen this wouldn't really do. Ambrose Scurl might be as remote and withdrawn as you please, but he wasn't a landscape or a bowl of fruit—or even Micklethwaite's Derby winner. He was a human being, and had now, indeed, risen and picked up that teacup with the evident intention of suggesting its replenishment by his daughter. He had to be brought in, and kept in, on the impending negotiation. '. . . to paint your portrait,' Bibury said.

'You are very kind, Sir Charles.' Scurl's features didn't much go in for any change of expression. It is characteristic of the depressive that he wears a mask. But now Scurl was looking at his interlocutor with a definite hint of surprise. It was clear that this was the first the man had heard of the thing, or at least the first occasion upon which he had permitted himself to register it. At the same time, he had spoken in a tone of extraordinary courtesy. Swinburne himself—Swinburne had for some reason been in Bibury's head—could not have received a proposal from

G. F. Watts with more of aristocratic graciousness. Bibury fleetingly wondered whether the Scurls—it was a dreadful name—had in fact come over with the Conqueror. 'If my memory does not betray me,' Scurl went on, 'nobody has taken my likeness hitherto.'

This was sufficiently old world, but academic rather than positively archaic. When you painted a Provost or a Principal or a President of some college or another the activity was likely to be described as 'taking a likeness' in such formal letters as you received. And that relevant words had been coaxed out of Scurl at all was something that Bibury found encouraging.

'There's just one small difficulty,' he went on. 'I've already mentioned it to your daughter. It's the matter of the time-element involved.'

'You have certainly mentioned *that*,' Mrs Blond said with a touch of asperity. It hadn't been of a 'small' difficulty that she had heard before, and she was probably now thinking that Bibury was having second thoughts as a consequence of her offering that fat cheque. 'But we are quite delighted,' she added instantly and cordially, 'that the thing will definitely come off.'

Bibury didn't much take to this. Mrs Blond, although doubtless an ornament of good society, was a commonplace and even slightly common little woman in comparison with her afflicted but distinguished father.

'It so happens,' Bibury went on, 'that within the next few days I have to be off to New York to fulfil a number of commissions. There's no getting out of it, and it's a matter of several months. But I'd get back as soon as I could—say by the end of May or the middle of June—and we'd get cracking. How about it?' Bibury was pleased with the briskness of these colloquial expressions, and also by the fact that he had now spoken the truth of the matter.

'You must in no way incommode yourself,' Scurl said. 'For have we not world enough and time?' This ought to have been encouraging, but was not so in fact. Its tone, although courteous still, had been without any warmth of interest. One simply had to remember, Bibury told himself, that despite an inflexible adherence to the forms Ambrose Scurl was never other than very far away. Or *down*—fathoms-deep in his smothering dejection. His daughter, on the other hand, was all there, and she immediately took up the running with the clear objective of pressing home what she saw as an advantage.

'But, Sir Charles,' she said, 'if you were able to delay your departure by a week or ten days, might the portrait not be achieved within that space of time? Of course I know little of such things.'

'That, my dear lady, I have to believe.' Bibury perhaps surprised himself by the severity of this response. But it was as if the woman had been about to propose paying him overtime—and as if, too, she had relegated his mystery to the mechanic employments. But was that quite the state of the case? Was she not prompted to her unseemly urging of haste by some tolerably legitimate apprehension? Bibury stole a searching glance at the sadly superannuated philosopher. Scurl was, of course, in extreme old age—or at least in what, even at the present day in his class and country, must be regarded as the next thing to it. In her letter the lady had frankly owned to this as a point of anxiety, so perhaps her father's health was under some threat that was not immediately apparent. Though not yet visibly wasting away, the man was undoubtedly haggard—a fact which possibly one was inclined to discount as attributable to his vastly obvious nervous condition. If there was danger here, it would be only humane to go easy with the lady.

'Unless we were thinking merely of a sketch,' Bibury therefore said, 'it really wouldn't do. It would be unfair both to the painter and to his subject.'

'Then we must dismiss the notion.' As usual, Mrs Blond was quick at tactical retreat. 'Only give us good notice, Sir Charles, of the date on which you will turn up. A room must be made ready for the work. That sort of thing.'

'Turn up?' The philosopher, who had been at his most melancholy-remote during these exchanges, suddenly spoke with a sharpness quite new in him. 'There will be no question of preparing a room. I will naturally wait on Sir Charles in his studio. The Rolls, my dear child, is extremely comfortable, and Graham is a most reliable man. There will be no difficulty at all.'

With this speech—and rather surprisingly—Ambrose Scurl got to his feet, bowed with gravity to his daughter's guest, shook hands, and walked from the room.

II

So in due season, and with Bibury's American commitments honourably behind him, the sittings began. But although the month was June—and in London a June as flawless as the month's elevated social character deserved—Ambrose Scurl appeared to have carried into it a rather wintry suggestion of cough and cold. The chauffeur called Graham, who shared with Scurl's butler his air of considerable sadness no doubt contracted by a species of infection from their employer, had to dive into that comfortable car and do a good deal of unsheathing of rugs and mufflers before the philosopher was decanted from it and ushered into Bibury's studio. And Scurl soon revealed himself as a testing sitter. It wasn't that he at all consciously 'posed'. He didn't preserve a sufficiently lively awareness of what was going on to be doing that. But there was something about him that came to almost the same thing. It was as if here were a professional model, a nude girl perched on a little dais, bored and with a high command of professionally acquired immobility. Bibury knew, of course, that in a sense this was what he was painting: a man absent from his surroundings, and from himself as well, for long stretches of time. Had Scurl in fact been a healthy young female innocently unclad in the interest of art this would have mattered very little. But serious portraiture cannot be achieved without some sort of rapport between artist and subject, and anything like that was substantially lacking. Fancifully, Bibury told himself that he would almost be resigned to catching the dumps of Graham and the butler if it would put him firmly on the same wave-length as Schopenhauer's Hampstead epigone. But this wasn't possible—simply because he was himself constitutionally disposed to look on the comfortable side of things.

He had naturally developed over the years a fairly extensive repertory of dodges for coping with one type of sitter or another. Stodgy ones, self-conscious ones, and those frozen up or uneasily exuberant: he had an adequate manner, appropriate chit-chat, for them all. Dead-silly women, and men who, finding themselves in what they judged to be a 'Bohemian' environment, indulged in lascivious reminiscences: he had no difficulty with these either. But Scurl was a tougher test. It wasn't that he was obstinately silent. If Bibury offered a commonplace remark, he frequently, although not invariably, received some sort of courteous response. As at his daughter's tea-table, Scurl's politeness was unfaltering without ever being awkwardly excessive.

'You must always say,' Bibury had explained on the occasion of the first sitting, 'if you want to take a bit of a breather. Being stared at can be rather a bore—and even a strain at times. It's the sense of being measured out in millimetres, I think. So do get up and wander round. There are just a few things in the studio that might interest you.'

'Thank you. I will avail myself of your kindness at need. How incredible that any rational man could have taken it into his head that our universe is the handiwork of an omnipotent and benevolent creator.'

So abrupt a dive into theology was disconcerting, but Bibury did his best to keep his end up in face of it.

'I suppose,' he said, 'that's what the Manichaeans felt they were coping with.'

'There is certainly much to be said for the view that Adam was Satan's supreme creation. It is most kind of you to have your servant entertain Graham to tea.' This further daunting inconsequence was succeeded by a long period of silence, and then Scurl spoke again. 'They contrived, you know, both to crucify him and to flay him alive. It must have been a considerable technical achievement, and constitutes—does it not?—a striking excess of the *odium theologicum*. But the Persians always go in for undue elaboration. Consider their carpets. Let me not neglect to transmit to you, my dear Sir Charles, my daughter's kind regards. Mani's thought was no doubt rashly syncretic. But the admonishments of the Magians were undeniably on the drastic side.'

It was only after three or four sittings that Bibury began to suspect that this wandering talk on the triste philosopher's part was linked to an increasing physical disability. The cough was gaining ground and had become positively sinister in suggestion. The sittings grew shorter—and patently on instructions received by Graham from Mrs Blond. A cheerless Graham would enter the studio with wraps over his arm, and that would be that. Bibury was at once acquiescent in this slightly unusual drill. Better the Rolls than an ambulance—or, for that matter, an undertaker's van. That last thought was almost certainly a product of undue alarm, since Bibury was intuitively aware that his sitter's physique was not of the kind that issues in a sudden dropping dead. But the man wasn't merely unwell; he was now wasting away. After a few more sessions Bibury was sure of it. He also saw that as the sittings grew shorter and were reduced to a couple in the week the exercise looked like extending itself over several months. He was, in fact, taking the likeness—endeavouring to keep up with the changing lineaments—of a patently dying man! At what point, he asked himself, was he to arrest on his canvas this process of dissolution? For how far ought he to call upon his art to pursue the mortal tenement of Ambrose Scurl within the obscuring, finally the obliterating shades? Such questions were bizarre indeed.

It occurred to him that his own involvement in whatever impended could be a little curtailed were he to adopt Mrs Blond's first notion that the sittings should take place in Hampstead. There was always a good deal of the vexatious in such an altered arrangement, particularly in regard to the changed lighting resulting from it. And there was awkwardness in speaking or writing to Scurl's daughter about such fresh dispositions. His own apprehensiveness over the philosopher's physical health was perhaps exaggerated, and might needlessly disturb the lady. He decided to bide his time.

The result was a period during which the philosopher's depressive state intensified. Steadily, he appeared to possess less and less even of surface awareness of what was going on. There were, of course, those expressions of courtesy. Such things are not required to have more than a modicum of feeling behind them. But with Scurl they now plainly had none at all. It was merely that, in early years about which Bibury possessed no information, standards of behaviour had been fed into the man, and now remained there when he was almost ceasing to be a man at all.

It was all the more disconcerting in that, just now and then, coherence and a fleeting command of intellectual concepts would emerge. Or Scurl would utter, but with a strange tonelessness, scraps of verse. They were most often by A.E. Housman, and occasionally by Thomas Hardy, or by some poet Bibury couldn't identify. 'Ashes under Uricon,' he might say obscurely. Or he would walk to a window—from which there was a charming view—and turn back to inform the painter that high heaven and earth ail from the prime foundation. Tempted to experiment, Bibury contrived to leave open on a table a volume reproducing some of Dürer's engravings. And Scurl did look at it.

'Ah,' Scurl said—but listlessly. 'Melancholy. The speculative intellect, though winged, is baffled amid the litter of its instruments. A powerful thing. I can recall being much taken by it when a child.'

'The *Melencolia I*,' Bibury said gently. 'There were to be two others, I believe, only Dürer never got round to them. I've read that he knew a lot about melancholy, and suffered periods of deep depression.' Bibury was ashamed of this fishing even as he indulged it. But Scurl had already turned away, as from something without significance. It was clear that the man wouldn't readily be tempted to exchange, so to speak, sitting behind a painter's easel for lying on an amateur psycho-analyst's couch. Bibury remembered the brandy and soda, and tried drink, although at a most inappropriate afternoon hour. Scurl accepted vodka without demur, but it made not the slightest difference to him. Bibury himself, on the other hand, it considerably upset. Such an experiment, freakish even if trivial, suggested that he was somehow becoming obsessed by his odd sitter. His hours with him were turning distinctly dispiriting. Thinking again of Graham and that butler, he realized that their employer wasn't merely gloomy himself. He was also, and insidiously, a cause of gloom in other men. The sooner one was shut of the dreary and ailing old chap the better. So Bibury pushed on with the portrait with as much speed as he could conscientiously contrive.

But soon there came a perplexing development. Scurl continued to ail—so rapidly and drastically that Bibury had to consider putting himself in communication with Mrs Blond with the aim of stopping the whole thing. But he felt that this course would be extremely difficult. It would be tantamount to saying to the woman: 'Look, your father's health is deteriorating so fast, and having so drastic an effect on his appearance, that I no longer know what I'm trying to put on my canvas.' It was a proposition so grotesque and unexampled (or, if exampled, never in an instance he had heard of) that he couldn't imagine himself by any means whatever articulating it to the lady. He even came to wonder whether it would not be best to feign illness or even permanent disability in himself. There were those terrible things that sometimes happened to an artist's eyes—to Degas's, for instance, or yet more terribly to Piero della Francesca's. But Bibury, unlike Piero, had no flair for mathematics. He would have to remain a painter, and one conscious of having told an innocent woman a thumping lie. Bibury was startled at finding himself nursing such stupid fantasies. But they persisted, and got in the way of his work.

It was through a vision thus at least metaphorically clouded that he presently became aware of a freshly disconcerting fact. Scurl, although he continued to ail, didn't continue consistently dreary. He began to go in for what could only be called fits—or at first no more than glints, gleams—of excitement. He chattered—briefly but alarmingly. On several occasions he produced incomprehensible jokes that were like wild laughter in the throat of death. Although latterly able to move only on Graham's arm, he would contrive to get on his feet unaided and totter with a kind of desperate curiosity round the studio. He managed to find the *Melencolia I* again, and was amused by what he called the 'doggie' contorted in it bottom-left. Bibury had thought of his sitter as permanently and, as it were, reliably sad. He now concluded that he was very much of the up-and-down sort. Bibury got hold of an appropriate textbook and read a chapter on manic-depressive psychosis. It was informative, but couldn't be called particularly wholesome stuff. He began—as everybody does who seeks instruction about such matters—a good deal to wonder about himself. He hadn't ever in his life felt less cheerfully disposed.

Thus perplexed and disturbed, he decided to turn to Graham. He had discovered that the chauffeur was of a good many years' standing as an employee in the Hampstead household—which indeed one might have guessed from the extent to which the man had become low-spirited himself. Contriving a private word with Graham wasn't easy, but Bibury managed it one afternoon when Scurl dropped surprisingly into an uneasy and cough-tormented sleep.

'I wouldn't like to worry Mrs Blond about her father,' Bibury began. 'But the professor doesn't seem to me to be at all well.'

'You're telling me. If it was curtains tomorrow, who'd say surprise, surprise?'

'Quite so. There's been a distinct deterioration even in the short time I've known him.' Bibury hadn't greatly cared for Graham's manner of speaking, but at least the man seemed willing to talk. 'And I fear it's really a question of whether the portrait should go on. Do you by any chance know whether Mrs Blond appears to have any such thought in mind?'

'A cow as couldn't see a gate in front of it, that woman is.'

Bibury of course found this remark extremely improper. But inwardly he had to agree that Mrs Blond was a strong-willed rather than a perceptive person. She had set her mind on the portrait, and it would take a lot to persuade her that it should be scrapped—or even finished, as would be perfectly proper, without the further attendance of its subject in the studio.

'I suppose, Graham, that the professor has always had his ups and downs? On the nervous side, if you follow what I mean.'

Graham didn't fail to indicate with a sardonic glance his awareness that he might be supposed too thick to understand a perfectly lucid distinction. But again he spoke up readily enough.

'No,' he said. 'No way, Sir Charles. It's five years I've been with him, and never a cheery chirp has he come up with until almost the other day. It gets you down, does having a fair chronic around year in, year out.'

'It hasn't got his daughter down.'

'I wouldn't say it doesn't tell on her. I've known her pretty sharp.'

'No doubt.' Bibury told himself he was doing very wrong in encouraging Graham to talk thus freely about his employers. But his principal impulse was to make sure that he had understood the man. 'Are you saying,' he asked, 'that in your experience the professor has been low spirited and depressed without interruption—until some change has come upon him in the last few weeks, and he has become—in wretched health though he be—capable of an almost buoyant tone?'

'Just that.'

'Have you any idea of what his daughter thinks about it?'

'He's pretty close with her still, the old chap is. But he talks to me.' Graham paused to glance cautiously at Ambrose Scurl, still slumbering at the other end of the studio. 'He makes plans for the two of us. First one plan and then another—and changing pretty rapidly. Just now it's that we're to be off to Monte Carlo in the Rolls together, and break the bank there. Because of what he calls his new theory of probability. A load of crap, I call that. There's still plenty of the philosopher about him, mark you. But now cheerfulness keeps breaking in.' Unconscious of thus quoting Dr Johnson's friend Mr Edwards, Graham shook his head pityingly. 'And only this morning, it was champagne and oysters at the Ritz.'

'Was *what*?'

'We are to say one day that we're doing a double stint here with you—and go to the Ritz together for champagne and oysters. Quite why them, I don't know. Nasty slimy things! The old fellow's notion of what they call dissipation, it may be. It's a dull life in Hampstead.'

'I suppose so.' Bibury was now anxious to bring this unseemly conversation to a close. 'I think I'd better wake him up—gently, of course—and finish up for the day.'

'Any day now will finish *him* up, if you ask me. That cough! It's like listening to the nails going into the coffin. It fair gets me down. And Jobbins too, for the matter of that.' Jobbins was the butler. 'And the old bastard's got *you* down, all right. Haven't I seen it. The two of you like a bloody see-saw these weeks past.'

'Not like a see-saw.' Bibury, although constrained to put up with bad language, couldn't accept this undignified image. 'But it's true that he has been—as you put it—getting me down of late, and himself up after a fashion. And now we'll say no more about it. I rather think I understand the state of the case.'

And more understanding followed rather quickly. Ambrose Scurl woke up, and Graham beat a brisk retreat.

'Dear me!' Scurl said. 'Have I been taking a nap? It's the result of feeling relaxed, you know. Having—did I tell you, Bibury?—finished the book.'

'You've been writing a book?' There was an understandable surprise in Bibury's tone.

'Well, not writing it, exactly. But it's all so clear in my head that it may be called as good as written. So time to take a holiday, eh? As you will do, my dear Bibury, when you've completed this admirable portrait.'

Hitherto Scurl had always said 'Sir Charles'. But now it was suddenly 'Bibury' in a cordial and entirely appropriate fashion. And Scurl, although coughing horribly and appearing to draw every breath with pain, managed to get to his feet and shamble round the studio.

'A cruise,' he said. 'That's what I'll go for. See things I ought to have seen long ago. Ancient cizilizations and other ways of living. All that.'

'One of those Hellenic affairs?' It seemed to Bibury that retired professors listening to other retired professors lecturing on the Minoans would be what Scurl had in mind in this painful fantasy.

'Well, no. Rather dull, all that—eh? One of the whacking great liners—why not the biggest of the lot?—doing a round-the-world affair. Months of it.'

'I see. But isn't that sort of set up . . .' Bibury was about to say 'a matter of atrociously vulgar gormandizing and chucking money around'. But he checked himself in time. 'Doesn't it tend to be a bit rackety?' he substituted.

'No harm in a bit of fun, Bibury—no harm at all.'

'Well, no—I suppose not. Will your daughter go with you?'

'My dear chap! She'd be wholly out of her element, bless her. Think of Bali.'

'Bali?'

'A little commercialized these days, no doubt. But the girls are said to be still marvellous—absolutely marvellous. Mind you, it will be no more than a holiday—although an extended one. A bit of a spree, eh? When I get back, I'll soon have a great deal of work on hand, a great deal of work. This book I've spoken of. No more than a parergon, Bibury, although a fairly weighty one. I have to face it, you know. The *magnum opus* has yet to come. *Finis coronat opus*—eh? The same thing's ahead of you also, I'd say. You'll have to get down to it, Bibury. Soul-destroying it must be, endlessly turning out tarted-up daubs of socialite nonentities. Where's Graham? Where's Graham, I say? We must be off, you know, we must be off.'

Under this sudden and urgent persuasion, Ambrose Scurl turned round all too hastily in search of his chauffeur. His legs gave way beneath him and he fell, a crumpled heap, to the floor. And Bibury saw that his mouth was gushing blood.

So there was occasion for an ambulance, after all. On the

following afternoon Bibury rang up Mrs Blond and made the proper inquiries.

'My father will come home from hospital on Friday or Saturday,' Mrs Blond said. 'It is all arranged. Nurses have been engaged, and Lord Pie has promised to look in every day.' Lord Pie was a very exalted physician indeed. 'So there need be no call for alarm.'

'That is excellent news.' Bibury wondered how fatuous this sounded. 'How is he bearing up? Is he in reasonably good spirits?'

'He is very buoyant and confident, I am glad to say.' Mrs Blond paused on this. 'When he is conscious, that is.'

'I see.'

'Lord Pie says that we must be just *ever so little* cautious over that. It appears that when the lungs are *tainted*—as I fear my father's have been for some time—there is a tendency in the patient to euphoric feeling and behaviour. To being rather optimistic, in fact.' Mrs Blond added this gloss as if mindful that an artist might well be unfamiliar with a learned word. 'Lord Pie says that it can often be a most *helpful* circumstance. So much is within the power of the mind, is it not?'

'Yes.' Bibury didn't very well know how to respond here. 'Quite so. Your father has certainly struck me just lately as commanding quite a stock of useful optimism. He was speaking, incidentally, of perhaps taking rather a long holiday. Do you think he might be persuaded to go to Switzerland—to Davos-Platz, or somewhere like that?'

'I think not.' Mrs Blond sounded displeased. 'Lord Pie assures me that sanatoria of the kind you probably have in mind are no longer considered *en règle*. But about the portrait, Sir Charles.' This came from the lady with much the effect of recalling the cobbler to his last. 'My father has mentioned it once or twice, saying it won't be at all difficult to resume the sittings soon.'

'But nothing of the kind will be in the least necessary.' Bibury provided this assurance with almost indecent haste and emphasis. Scurl, he now clearly realized, had really succeeded in making him miserable, and he never wanted to see the man again. 'There are things still to be done to it, of course. But they don't in the least require the professor's presence. Please tell him so.'

'Very well, but I fear he will be disappointed. Only this morning, he remarked that you and he had been having some jolly chats. And just before dozing off—or *lapsing*, perhaps I should say—he said something about *bally*-somewhere. I failed to follow him. Might he have been thinking of some place in Ireland?'

'I have no idea, Mrs Blond. No idea at all. And now I must not detain you longer. You must have much to do and think about. Do, please, give my good wishes to the professor—and perhaps you will ring me up later, and tell me how things go.'

'In a week or ten days' time, Sir Charles.' This was again Mrs Blond putting a superior kind of hireling in his place—or so Bibury construed it. 'For the present, goodbye.'

It was, in fact, only after quite a long interval that Mrs Blond rang up. She did so early one morning.

'Sir Charles?' she said, 'this is Muriel Blond. My father would very much like to see you. Please come.'

'But of course.' Bibury said this from an instant feeling that the woman was upset and ought to be deferred to. The words didn't at all correspond to his inward feeling about Ambrose Scurl.

'It's about a frame.'

'I beg your pardon?'

'About a frame for the portrait. It seems to be worrying my father very much. About the sort of frame the National Portrait Gallery would approve of. He feels you ought to know.'

'I see.' What Bibury (whose nervous tone was still obstinately astray) thought he saw was a monstrous impertinence. That he should be haled out to Hampstead to talk to a sick man about a picture-frame! If it wasn't impertinent, it was certainly absurd. 'I'm afraid that, just at present . . .'

'My father is very upset, Sir Charles, and able to talk very little. But the frame does seem to worry him. I am worried myself, but needn't say it's not about that. When Lord Pie came in yesterday, he said that there must undeniably be some small occasion for anxiety. It's something he has never said before. Such a confident man! And I must confess that your little journey may be in vain. My father sleeps a great deal. I have heard the nurses talking together about coma. They are only ignorant women, of course. But it *was* Lord Pie himself who recommended them.'

'I see. Shall I come out straight away, or would it be better in the afternoon?'

'Oh, thank you, Sir Charles, thank you! The mid-afternoon, I think. He is sometimes a little clearer then.'

'Good! Say three o'clock. And I expect I can find a few bits and pieces—of frames, that is—that might interest your father. Goodbye.'

Bibury hung up, and went into his studio. The portrait was there—finished and stacked with its face to the wall. He hadn't looked at it since satisfied that there was nothing more to be done, and he didn't much want to look at it now. He was no longer clear in his head about what he would find on the canvas if he turned it round. Had he simply painted the courteous depressive whom he had first encountered over Mrs Blond's *petits fours*? Or had he caught Scurl as he began to pass into the final phase of what must have been a long-established wasting disease? Or had he, during the last stretch of his labours, evoked by certain deft strokes of the brush that dreadful state of roseate and fatuous day-dream which the Dark Angel ironically induces in this sort of sufferer when preparing to seize upon his prey? Or was it conceivable that Charles Bibury, R.A., had arrived at a third manner after all; had penetrated beneath the mere flux and mutability of things to whatever is unchanging and indestructible in an individual human spirit? Bibury put out his hand to the canvas. Then he thought better of this, ate an uneasy luncheon, and called a taxi.

He rummaged out some meaningless bits and pieces of gilded wood, and put them in a bag. Then—surely grotesquely—he changed into a dark suit, and was ready for his painful mission. He would speak to Ambrose Scurl, without false cheerfulness but not sorrowfully either, and with what he could manage of sober attention to the hypothetical predilections of the National Portrait Gallery. He would talk for an appropriate length of time in this way, whether Scurl bore any appearance of hearing him or not.

But it wasn't to be. A short and well-kept drive led up to the Hampstead house: imposing and four-square, with two large windows on either side of a portico, five windows above these, and five identical windows above that again. Fourteen windows. And in every one of them a blind had been drawn down.

'Stop!' Bibury's order to the taxi-driver was peremptory, and the man was so startled that he brought the cab to a halt with a jolt and a jerk. It was only very briefly that Bibury had then to hesitate. He was in no degree an intimate of the stricken household in front of him, and to turn his proposed professional visit into one of awkward and premature condolence would be of no help to Muriel Blond. 'You can see what has happened,' Bibury said. 'Something on which I mustn't intrude. Take me back.'

'It's up to you,' the man said. And he reversed down the drive.

As soon as he got home, Bibury wrote the proper sort of letter. He posted it that evening. At dinner he uncorked a bottle of good claret, and drank half of it. But he failed to sleep at all well. He found himself worrying about that taxi-driver. Had the man felt—without knowing the first thing about the situation—that his fare had somehow behaved inadequately? It was an odd sort of discomfort to lie awake with. During many succeeding days Bibury felt increasingly out of sorts, and finally he had to acknowledge fully what he had been intermittently conscious of for some time: that he had caught from Scurl a bug having nothing to do with tuberculosis. He mightn't have captured on canvas the philosopher's melancholy condition, but in a formidable sense it had captured him. Eventually Bibury saw his doctor, and was given some pills. But Christmas had come and gone by the time he felt quite up to the mark again.

TOM DICK AND HARRY

'THEY MUST BE told sooner or later,' Arthur Patchett said to his wife. 'And the sooner the better, I'd suppose. When it still won't mean very much to them.'

'I've been thinking.' Muriel Patchett spoke as if this was a rather uncommon event. 'Need they *ever* know? Even now, it might be upsetting. And when we are all getting along so well together.'

'Certainly we're doing *that*. There's not a doubt about it.' Arthur pronounced this with all the authority proper in a successful business man. 'But the time will come when the state of the case must be brought into the open. I understand there's an age at which a young person acquires the legal right to see any relevant documents there may be. You and I think of Tom, Dick and Harry as still no more than kids who wouldn't make much even of a birth certificate shoved under their noses. But they're growing older every day, aren't they?' Patchett paused on this, much as if it were a proposition which his wife might be moved to dispute. 'And nowadays there are several quite trivial situations in which a young adult has to produce such a certificate. Or at an earlier age a boy may simply gather that such documents exist, and ask to see his own out of mere curiosity. If that were to happen with us, and it became obvious that we had been withholding information about our family set-up instead of being candid about it, the result might well be what you call upsetting.'

The circumstances giving rise to this conversation were not at all complicated. Arthur and Muriel Patchett, having waited in vain through several years after their marriage for parenthood to come to them, had adopted a male infant upon whom they bestowed the name of Thomas. Hard upon their so doing, Muriel became pregnant—which was not, it appeared, an unusual sequel to an act of adoption. She was then delivered of male twins, and to these the parents somewhat unguardedly gave the names of Richard and Henry. It was thus that Tom,

Dick and Harry Patchett came into the world. There were no further Patchett children.

Dick and Harry were identical twins—'monozygotic' the doctor had learnedly said—and it was, of course, regularly declared by all who came into contact with them that they were as like as two peas. And, oddly enough, Tom, who was senior to the twins by little more than a year, bore a marked physical resemblance to them, although there was no possibility of any blood-tie being in question. From time to time acquaintances even spoke of them as the Patchett triplets, and since Arthur and Muriel inclined to reticence in the matter, this further misconception went largely uncontradicted. Moreover, it had so happened that shortly after the birth of the twins Arthur Patchett moved his activities and abode from the south of England to the north. The society into which the Patchetts were thus brought took little interest in family relationships and what may be called lineage. The women talked mostly about the cost of clothes and comestibles, the men about motor cars and the threatening incomprehensibilities of a rapidly developing computerized world. Had the Patchetts contrived a multiple birth—six or seven at a go such as one occasionally sees on television—the progress of the litter would have been watched with some curiosity. But twins were of no particular interest, and triplets, although more of a rarity, were equally without much news value. All this was satisfactory to Arthur and Muriel as they continued to hesitate about coming clean to the three boys.

Then—but a good many years later—a new factor emerged. All three were eventually sent to the same school: a grammar school of some note which had lately become 'independent' and cost parents a good deal of money. Having two, or even three, sons at the school simultaneously was a form of conspicuous expenditure rather admired by the community at large. What emerged from this set-up, however, was an institution providing rigorous academic training for a minority of clever boys in part financed through the intake of a majority of 'thickies' (as they were occasionally called by the masters in their common-room) whose best chance of distinction lay within the field of athletic prowess. The school was thus a somewhat polarized place.

It certainly polarized the young Patchetts. In no time at all, those masters who prided themselves as early spotters of talent were predicting an Oxford scholarship for Tom Patchett. Contrastingly, Dick and Harry—Tom's younger twin brothers as the school understood them to be—might, if they took their rugger seriously, end up with the modest distinction of playing for the Second Fifteen.

So here was sibling jealousy in the making. The three boys were no longer 'getting along well' either with each other or with the senior Patchetts. The culprit initially was Tom, without a doubt. A strain of arrogance (inherited from heaven knew whom) was becoming more and more apparent in him. Precocious in his reading as in almost everything else, he had found a poem that spoke of the flannelled fools at the wicket and the muddied oafs at the goals, and this he chanted gleefully at Dick and Harry, without much regarding the context in which Kipling had placed the lines. But Dick and Harry were quickly at fault too. That they were younger than Tom was by this time scarcely apparent as a matter of physique, and they were also two to one. 'Scrag him!' they would shout each to the other, and a very ill-tempered rumpus would follow.

Arthur Patchett was upset. There was positively bad blood between the boys—and at times actual blood as well from a cut lip or a punched nose. In fact Arthur no longer presided over anything like a happy family. Moreover, his wife had ceased to feel that the true relationship between the three boys should be concealed through an indefinite future. She wanted the truth to be revealed *now*. The parents had thus exchanged grounds.

'But, Muriel,' her husband said just after there had been a particularly disagreeable dispute between Tom and his suppositious brothers, 'I think I was right quite a long time ago in feeling that the situation should be explained then and there, when they were all three too young to know that it was anything very unusual or to be bothered about. But now we're in a particularly sticky phase. Tom and the twins have got up against each other, and it's largely due to some kind of rivalry between them that has developed at school. Give them a little time, and they'll get over it. This is precisely *not* the moment to come out with the thing.'

'I don't see that. But I do see that it's something to do with the school. Tom is better at his books. All that silly Latin and maths come much more easily to him than to our own children.'

Arthur Patchett was silent for some moments. When Muriel had said 'our own children' she was breaking a kind of taboo long since agreed between them. But it was true, Arthur had to admit, that Dick and Harry *were* their own children, which Tom in a radical way was not. And Muriel was more likely to be constantly aware of the fact than he was. It was without any birth-pangs that Tom had come to them.

Made sharply aware of this, Arthur prolonged his silence. He may be said even to have searched his own heart. Was there going to be a rift in the family—and a rift in which he and his wife were to be on opposite sides? It ought to be possible to regard such a situation as inconceivable. But it looked like being true. To begin with something unimportant yet with a lurking significance, it wouldn't readily come to him to speak of Latin and maths as 'silly'. He was a sound business man, and had a sound business man's respect for ability wherever he found it. Such a man was likely to be as pleased as Punch on discovering that some young clerk he had imported into his office was proving to possess abilities or aptitudes that were likely to take him right up the ladder. He himself had never had a Latin grammar in his hands, and his sums were done for him on machines. But it pleased him to think of Tom as likely to go to Oxford and shine there.

'I'm not at all sure,' he now heard his wife say, 'that it wouldn't do Tom good to be taken down a bit. He's becoming conceited, if you ask me.'

'I know what you mean, my dear. But I'm inclined to think that "conceited" isn't quite the word for the boy. He's simply becoming conscious of his own endowments.'

'Yes—and that they're going to take the shine off Dick and Harry. I don't at all like that in the family.'

'Of course not. But aren't you being a little unfair to Tom? I agree that he has a pride that may lead him into trouble. But he's up against these slightly younger brothers—as he supposes them to be—who are good at games, and so on; in fact at the kind of things that the majority of schoolboys particularly admire. And I'm not sure that Dick and Harry don't physically humiliate Tom at times. Acting together, they have almost twice the muscular equipment that he has.' Arthur Patchett made one of his frequent pauses, as if surprised by the words and sentiments he had heard himself uttering. 'Muriel,' he then said, 'we must be extremely careful. It's clear to me that Tom must indeed be told about the manner of his coming to us. And told quite soon. But behind the stating of the facts there mustn't be the slightest hint that we are telling him—well, that he is no son of ours.'

For a short period after this discussion Arthur Patchett felt able to tell himself that it had in a thoroughly wholesome fashion cleared the air. The three boys, of course, knew nothing about it, and the rift between them remained unaltered. But Muriel, who had for some time contrived to have little to say to Tom, seemed to have taken her husband's brief homily to heart, and now talked to her adopted son quite a lot. Tom, on his part, seemed on his way to conquering, or at least abating, the irritating arrogance that had lately possessed him. It was perhaps—Arthur thought—because things were going well with him at school; he had been awarded a prize for an essay on Oliver Cromwell, and had begun to contribute to the school magazine. So it was out of an almost clear sky that the thunderbolt came.

'Please show me my birth certificate.'

Tom had walked into a room called for some reason the study, in which Arthur Patchett was accustomed to smoke a pipe and read a newspaper after the evening meal. Tom had given a formal knock on the door, and on opening it had wasted few words.

It was as bad a moment as had befallen Arthur for a long time. Either his wife had disregarded what had been in all but its phraseology a command, or she had badly underestimated

Tom's ability to draw an accurate conclusion from some ambiguous phrase or hint of a mystery. Probably it was the second of these conjectures that was correct. It was possible, too, that Tom had for long a little wondered about himself. That he chanced to bear a considerable physical likeness to the twins might have militated against any distinct sense of his being among the Patchetts a kind of cuckoo in the nest. But consanguinity or the absence of it may intimate itself intuitively at some deep level of the mind, and thence erupt into consciousness upon some quite slender prompting occasion. All this Arthur Patchett dimly knew. He was reflecting on it as the boy briefly studied the document which had been extracted from a locked drawer by the man whom he had been brought up to address as Father.

'It's not all that informative,' Tom said. 'But it's enough for a start. I'm no Patchett. That's what it comes to, isn't it?'

It was almost as if, at fifteen, Tom had suddenly grown up; and before his bald question Arthur, as might be expected, was extremely distressed. Muriel and he between them, he felt, had made a shocking mess of things. He had known, he repeated to himself, that from the earliest age at which Tom could understand what he was being told, his position as an adopted child ought to have been made clear to him, and then steadily treated as of no account in point of the normal loyalties and sanctities of family life. So much, at this critical moment, Arthur understood clearly. But just what was he to say to Tom *now*? What he did say was bound to be well intentioned, since he was steadily a well-intentioned man. He knew this to be so, and he plucked a certain measure of confidence from knowing it. And in that confidence he spoke.

'Tom,' he said, 'dear Tom, you mustn't feel *let down*. I know it's hard, but you must stick to the knowledge that we think of you in every way just as we think of Dick and Harry. We're one family, however we came to be so. And we'll stay that way.'

'Dick and Harry don't know? They've been as ignorant as I've been?'

'They certainly don't know—my dear, dear boy.'

'Then I'm going to be the first to tell them.'

As he said this, Tom tossed the fatal scrap of paper to the floor and turned and left the room.

Left to himself, Arthur Patchett dropped in a kind of stupor into his chair. The mess was worse than ever, and he groaned as he felt that the situation had passed entirely out of his control. He was still in this condition when, some ten minutes later, the study door opened and his wife came in. So, too, did a great deal of noise from an upper region of the house: so much noise, in fact, that Muriel had to shout to make herself heard.

'Whatever is it?' she demanded. 'Arthur, what have you done?'

'I've told Tom about himself. I had to. He'd pretty well found out. You must have——' Arthur checked himself. 'And he said he was going to tell the twins.'

'Listen! I suppose *that's* Tom telling them?' Even as Muriel spoke, the disturbance upstairs changed its character. There was rather less shouting. But now there came a kind of pounding and bumping that shook the ceiling above the senior Patchetts' heads.

'They're fighting,' Muriel said. 'Worse than ever, by the sound of it. And all because you——' Muriel, in turn, checked herself. 'You must go up and stop them.'

Thus challenged, Arthur did get to his feet and move uncertainly towards the door. But the door opened before he reached it, and Dick Patchett stumbled into the room, revealing to his agitated parents a bloodied nose and a bunged-up eye.

'What's going on?' Dick shouted. 'What the hell's going on? What rubbish have you been chucking at Tom? It *is* rubbish, isn't it? We've been telling him so, and—and trying to enforce the bloody argument. But Tom's mad. Tom's gone mad, I tell you!' Dick paused for a moment to apply a grubby handkerchief to his injured eye. 'He's always been pretty tough. It has taken Harry and me all we've got to do a bit more than hold our own with him. But now he's strong like he never was before. He's licked both of us! That's madness, isn't it?'

At this point Harry Patchett tumbled into the study in his turn, shouting as he did so.

'Just what's cooking?' Harry demanded. 'Tom says he's not our brother. Bloody hell, he's not! He has always been our brother, and he always will be. And he has more brains than the rest of us all put together. I told him he was talking a load of crap, and he went and knocked one of my teeth out! I never thought he had it in him! He *has* gone off his head, hasn't he?'

'Yes, hasn't he?' Dick echoed. 'He's still our brother, isn't he—even if he's gone completely bonkers? He says he's clearing out. I got him one you can guess where when he said that. But then he said it again. I think he's packing.'

'Both of you go to your rooms at once.' Arthur Patchett had summoned to his aid all the remnants of his authority. Ghastly as the mess was, he could, he felt, still control his own children. The boy—or youth—called Thomas Patchett was another matter; was suddenly become an unknown quantity or quality with whom a new relationship would have to be worked out. 'Have a thorough wash,' he amplified, 'and take care not to bloody the towels. Then go to bed, and be equally careful about the sheets. We'll talk about all this in the morning.'

Suddenly obedient but still bewildered, the Patchett twins took their departure from their father's study. For some seconds Arthur and Muriel gazed at one another wordlessly, and then Muriel spoke.

'They'll never forgive us,' Muriel said.

'For allowing a cuckoo in the nest?'

'Arthur, try not to be so *stupid*!'

His wife, Arthur thought, must be much overwrought to utter so senseless—indeed, so outrageous—an injunction. He must go carefully with her.

'My dear,' he said mildly, 'just what do you mean?'

'That they're *fond* of Tom. They *admire* him. If Tom really goes away, Dick and Harry—well, Dick and Harry won't like it at all. They'll feel disgraced, and that you and I are disgraced too.'

'Tom won't go away. He's too young to find himself a job.

And, apart from ourselves, he has nobody else in the world to turn to.'

'That's perfectly true.'

This came from Tom—Thomas Patchett as he perfectly legally was—who had appeared suddenly in the room with them. He was pale; like Dick he was going to have a spectacular black eye; as if some antagonist were still before him, his right hand guarded his crotch. But despite this indecorous oddity, he was evidently entirely in command of himself.

'Yes,' he said composedly. 'That is the position entirely.'

'We were given to understand you were packing,' Arthur Patchett said—and was instantly horrified by the feeble tone of jocularity he had sought to take refuge in.

'I've had second thoughts about that . . . *sir*.' It was at once apparent that all Tom's arrogance had returned to him. He took his right hand from where it had rested, stooped, and picked up the scrap of official documentation that still lay on the carpet. 'As I remarked before,' he said, 'it isn't all that informative. But perhaps I can find out more when I've learnt the ropes. Meanwhile, I'll stay with you—with all four of you—and help you in any way I can. Not to worry, sir. Not to worry, Mrs Patchett. I can manage with those two boys, you know. Common clay, certainly. But there's something that's nice enough about them.'

Momentarily at least, neither Arthur nor Muriel found a word to say. Unversed in psychiatry, they were ignorant of being in contact with what modern mad doctors have called the Myth of the Birth of the Hero.

'And now,' Tom said, 'I think I'll go to bed. But remember: it's only four Patchetts that are going to wake up tomorrow morning. *Gaudeamus igitur*.'

'And just what does that mean?' Arthur asked.

'It means that we can rejoice that it's just that way. Good night.'

THE DYSLEXIA FACTOR

I

Le nez de Cléopâtre: s'il eût été plus court, toute la face de la terre aurait changé. The thought is offered to us by Pascal, and is more or less echoed by Pope when he reflects on what mighty contests rise from trivial things.

I begin my narrative like this by way of owning—or shall I say merely making clear?—that although I have earned my living as a scholar of sorts I am essentially no more than a belletrist: one who potters about the byways of literature offering such amiable remarks as he can. I am therefore ill-equipped to enter into any scientific field whatever, let alone to render verisimilar and convincing a sequence of untoward events requiring for their adequate exposition a good deal of physiology, neurology, endocrinology, and things of that sort. But I must do my best—simply because sheer chance decreed my presence at what I am convinced was the seminal moment, the very *fons et origo*, of a distinctly fateful affair: of a 'trivial thing', in fact, that came to threaten upheaval potentially comparable with anything effected by Cleopatra's nose in the world of Mark Antony and Octavius Caesar.

So there, for a start, is a confessional paragraph. I can at least try to be a conscientious historian.

As a boy, and for a brief period, I had two very intelligent acquaintances. The first was called Martin Brand, and the second I never came to know other than by his surname, which was Howe. Martin and I were day-boys together at a preparatory school in Oxford, and we were intimates for perhaps a couple of years. Then Martin gained a scholarship to Winchester, while I went to my father's less intellectually distinguished public school. At once we dropped entirely out of one another's lives: partly because of this, and partly because my family went to live in Hull, where my father, having abandoned hope of further advancement at Oxford, had become a professor in some branch of mediaeval literature. Whether to go, or not to go, had produced quite a pother among us: a fact worth mentioning since it instances the very compassable concerns which alone came within my experience until, in middle age, I ran into the alarming events I now propose to relate. That I simply forgot about Martin Brand in the interval is the more remarkable in that, as a boy, he had made a strong if obscure impression on me. He wasn't in any common sense a rebel; at our prep school he was so busy coming top in everything that his behaviour was as conformist as might be; when he went eventually to Cambridge he may have become for a time a wild or angry young man; if so, I never heard anything about it. But I can only say that as, still in shorts, we mucked around together, I had a dim sense of him as nursing what I have to call an anarchic streak inside.

Howe was our gardener: a jobbing gardener, who was the Brands' gardener too. He came to each of us for a day a week. The Brands lived in North Oxford in what used to be called a college house. It owned a trim sort of garden, which was fairly spacious as gardens in prosperous suburbs go. We lived rather further out, in a rambling old house which was at least my father's property, not far from Water Eaton. There was a large and straggling garden, which on three sides merged in a formless and unplanned fashion into some five acres of untidy woodland. We called this the copse, and seldom did anything about it, so that at periods of rank growth our situation became something like Macbeth's in Dunsinane when Birnam Wood appeared to bestir itself against him. One of Howe's duties was to defend some sort of perimeter against this assault: a task which he performed with great vigour. I can still recall his triumphant shout of 'We're winning!' as he drove one of his machines through a final thirty feet of nettle and briar and bramble. There was an occasion upon which, knowing himself to be faced with a particularly hard day's work, he arrived accompanied by three grown-up sons, all of them in the army, who instantly stripped themselves to the waist in the garden-shed and fell to well-coordinated labour. I think I am right in saying that these emergency reinforcements came free of charge.

A certain sense of the mysterious attached to Howe. Occasionally he would ring us up from what seemed not to be a call-box in order to propose one altered arrangement or another. But if he had a telephone of his own he never offered us its number. How he had come to us in the first place I have forgotten or perhaps never knew; and I have an impression that we didn't even have a note of his address. From time to time, and always without explanation, he would fail to turn up for a fortnight or even three weeks on end. When this happened I would annoy my parents by maintaining that Howe was on the bottle again, or even briefly in gaol. It was then that my father would insist on Howe's notable intelligence—apparently believing that intelligence, sobriety and law-abidingness go habitually together. There was certainly no doubt about what we would then have called his I.Q. He thought clearly and quickly, and had a capacious memory for horticultural detail, as well as a great deal of useful lore in the field. Moreover, he appeared to have what may be termed a studious streak. In sunny weather he would eat his midday sandwiches while sitting on a chair outside his shed, with a newspaper, not of the most popular sort, spread out on a box before him. He once told me—and I think I recall the phrase accurately—that he was a 'perusing' man. Occasionally I noticed that the newspaper was considerably out-of-date. I assumed that he was catching up.

I ought to have mentioned that Martin Brand and I were not much interested in 'organized' games. To be laboriously 'coached' in the nets, and told to keep on watching the ball from the instant it left the bowler's hand and act accordingly, struck us as a stupid way of spending time. And since our school was not exigent in this regard, we spent a good deal of leisure loitering in our garden or his—sometimes, indeed, casually playing French cricket, and sometimes—perhaps a shade shame-facedly—resorting to Cowboys and Indians. We were so employed one day in my own garden when my father called me to his study window. He was about to hurry off in his car to a faculty meeting, and had taken it into his head to scribble down on the back of an envelope some instructions which he told me to hand to Howe. He seldom gave Howe any instructions at all, but now for some reason had decided that one task was to be perfomed before another, and both of these before a third. Probably my mother, who gave more thought to the garden than he did, had prompted him to the unusual action. This would account for the fact that he thought it proper to be emphatic about the thing. 'And just make sure he understands,' my father said, and turned away to stuff some papers into a brief-case. So Martin and I went off together in search of Howe. We found him whetting a scythe. Scything, already a dying art, was one of Howe's accomplishments.

'Please, Mr Howe,' I said—for I had been taught all about courtesy to servants and retainers—'my father has asked me to give you this.' I handed over the envelope. 'He was in a hurry, but I hope it's fairly clear.'

That Howe hesitated for a moment was Martin's impression, not mine. I was simply aware of his taking the envelope and glancing at it.

'Very good, Master Leonard,' he said. 'I'll see to it.' And he took up his whetstone again.

'What has Mr Burton asked you to do first, Mr Howe?' It was Martin who asked this, and, although he did so with a great air of simply seeking something to chat about, I found it distinctly odd—and odd, too, was something suddenly intent in Martin's glance from one to the other of us. As for Howe himself, he was, as the cliché has it, momentarily disconcerted. There could be no doubt about that. It is my clearest recollection of the incident.

'That's as may be,' Howe then said sharply, and gave the blade of the scythe a long flowing stroke. 'Any chance, there's plenty to do. So you'd better both be off.'

This was unceremonious, but not much out of order, particularly to myself. Howe and I were on familiar terms; he allowed me to ride the impressive motor-mower which I probably regarded as the Burtons' most prestige-conferring possession; in return I would fetch him cheese or tobacco or cigarette-papers from the village shop. Moreover, being both learned and clever, he was capable of instructing me on various aspects of the natural world which schoolmasters know nothing about. So I was displeased with Martin as we walked away.

'What did you ask him that for?' I demanded. 'It wasn't any business of yours what my father wrote to him.'

'*Wrote* to him,' Martin said. 'Exactly! You silly drip—didn't you *see*? Howe can't read. It's a discovery.'

'Can't read? Do you mean he needs spectacles? I've never seen him with any.'

'Spectacles my aunt.' Our vocabulary at that time was much influenced by the archaic pages of the *Magnet* and the *Gem*. 'The man's illiterate—and probably has all sorts of cunning wheezes to conceal the fact.'

'That must be nonsense. Everybody nowadays goes to one snot school or another and learns the three Rs. And Howe is highly intelligent: my father says so. Howe couldn't have missed out on learning to read. Nobody can, unless they're what's called ESN.'

'Howe's illiterate, Burton my child. Just as you are innumerate, and likely to remain so.'

'What do you mean—innumerate?' I asked indignantly. The term was new to me, and I suspected that what was being called into question was my dawning sexual maturity.

'Statistics, for one thing. I don't suppose you've as much as heard of them.' Martin, I imagine, already saw himself as booked to become a high-powered scientist. 'They'd tell you that quite a large number of people leave school unable to read well—or even to read at all. Of course, a large number of people can be quite a small percentage of *everybody*. But it seems there's a puzzle, all the same.'

'A puzzle, Martin?'

'Yes, a puzzle.' Martin Brand was suddenly dismissive; he was always wary of getting out of his depth. 'I'll look into it one day. Is your mother going to give me tea?'

'I suppose so,' I said ungraciously. I was conscious that

something had much disturbed me in this small episode. Just what it had been, or at what precise point it had occurred, I couldn't at all clearly see. But I carried away an odd and inconsequent picture of a malicious child who had suddenly seen how he can push you into the swimming-pool or tumble you off your bike. Something like that: a trivial thing—but potent, all the same.

II

Hull paid off, so far as my father was concerned. Comfortably ensconced there, 'teaching' something that nobody within a hundred miles of the place much wanted to hear about, he became within a mere decade its prime authority in England, so that we were back in Oxford in what was, in fact, my own final year as an undergraduate. After that, I had a longish spell in London, working for a crammer and doing a number of small things in a literary way. During this period my father died (something Oxford professors very seldom seem to do) and my mother went to live in Budleigh Salterton, so that I ceased to have any connection with the place. But then, and again after an interval, I found myself what may be called a niche there. It wasn't a university job, being merely something to do with the British Council. But by that time I had also established myself as a minor littérateur at large in the Sunday newspapers. And the dons of my old college, finding themselves one afternoon in a conclave with nothing much to occupy them, took it into their heads that I was deserving of an occasional square meal, and elected me to membership of their senior common room. It turned out that I had to pay for the square meals when I ate them, but it was an agreeable privilege, all the same. Moreover, having picked up in childhood some notion of the kind of chit-chat favoured on such occasions, I came to move freely if in a modest way in donnish circles generally, and it was thus that I revived my memory of, and casual acquaintance with, the companion of my youth.

Martin Brand was rather grand—or so a rhyme that went the rounds not unreasonably declared. He had become, in his vigorous prime, Galen Professor of Physike and Chirurgerie. In other words, he was bang up to date as Oxford's top medical man. But although this made him vastly eminent, he was known to be decently unassuming about it. He delivered an occasional lecture to the medical students, and this always ended with the injunction: '*Les malades, toujours les malades!*'—a favourite precept, it seemed, of a colleague equally eminent in France, insisting that no medical luminary, whatever his wattage, should fail to spend time at the bedside of the afflicted. This strictly clinical zeal took Martin himself to the bedside of a good many profitable private patients. There was a story, several times repeated to me, that thus summoned to the extreme north of Scotland at several guineas a mile, he had given as his professional opinion on a ducal sufferer that his Grace might get better, or might get worse, or might remain the same. It is not, on the whole, about unpopular characters that dons fabricate such stories or air such chestnuts. Martin was, I judged, very generally liked as a man in whom there was a good deal more than transpired over a glass of port. Dons are commonly thought of as rather a tame lot. If it be so, the fact may account for their being drawn to individuals in whom some aggressive or aberrant impulse is felt to lurk. And that was certainly the case with Martin. Something that I had sensed in him as a boy was still there. It had, as it were, sunk deeper inside, and thereby become more difficult to put a name to. But perhaps it had strengthened as well.

One night I chanced to dine as a guest of someone who was a fellow of the college to which Martin's Chair was attached in the odd Oxford fashion, and I found myself sitting next to my old schoolfellow at High Table. Or, rather, standing next to him, as we hadn't yet sat down. Grace had to be said before we could do that, and the grace was rather an elaborate affair. A servant would bellow for silence, whereupon the Provost, at one end of the table, would say a number of things in Latin. The senior fellow present, having taken his place at the other end, would interject a number of remarks in reply—also, of course, in the learned tongue. The performance, vaguely akin to a kind of badminton or pat-ball tennis, would continue for a minute or so, and then everybody (including some two hundred young men in the body of the hall) would sit down and fall to. But on this occasion there was a hitch. The Provost hadn't turned up, so the Pro-Provost had taken his place. And the Pro-Provost didn't know his stuff. This oughtn't to have mattered at all, since the entire pious rigmarole was printed on a thing like a ping-pong bat in front of him. He was in difficulty, nevertheless, and fell to mumbling. At this an undergraduate shouted, 'Louder!' (and was instantly, no doubt, identified by the bawling servant, and consequently fined a pound next day). A second undergraduate then shouted, '—and funnier!' (a hoary old joke likely to cost him the same sum). The situation might have got out of hand had not the senior fellow, with much presence of mind, firmly articulated, '*In saeculo saeculorum, Amen*', and sat down.

Everybody at High Table took care to be discreetly amused by this small contretemps. Or everybody except Professor Brand. He, having given me a brisk nod of recognition, produced a gesture of dismay.

'By God, Leonard! he said. 'It looks as if the Pro-Pro has got it as well. A bit too much, that is. And I thought I was in luck.'

'My dear Martin, whatever are you talking about?'

'Something confidential. I'll tell *you*—but don't breathe a word.' It might have been expected that this injunction would have been delivered in a lowered voice, but it wasn't my impression that Martin had taken any such prudent course. He was excited, and apparently much perturbed. 'The Provost's in the Acland,' he said, 'and under my care.' The Acland was a nursing home. 'But he doesn't want it known.'

'Good heavens, Martin! Has the man been stricken by a retributive disease?'

This was a tasteless joke, of which I was immediately ashamed. But Martin took it in his stride.

'A reasonable guess,' he said. 'But I doubt whether the old boy would much distinguish himself in the stews. But he does feel that, in a scholar, it's a particularly awkward thing.'

'Then just what is "it"?' I asked.

'Something right up my street. That's why I thought I was in luck when he came shambling in on me. But now the Pro-Provost too! What if the bloody condition spreads, and I can do damn-all about it? I'll be a laughing-stock.' And Martin glowered round the High Table almost as if he thought that this might already be the state of affairs.

'*Les malades, toujours les malades*,' I said. 'You will be able to hop from one bedside to the other. But explain.'

'You remember Howe?'

'Howe?' I echoed. For the moment the name conveyed nothing to me.

'You must remember Howe. The dyslectic gardener.'

'Dyslectic?' Again I was at sea. Had Martin found occasion to employ a word like 'dyslogistic' I'd have understood him at once. I am, as I have explained, a literary man.

'For pity's sake! "Word blindness", if you like. Howe couldn't read, and the disability had almost certainly been with him from the cradle. He had grown quite cunning about it.'

'I do remember now. But are you telling me that your Provost is dyslectic too? It must be quite unusual surely, for a man to become head of an Oxford college without ever having mastered his ABC.'

'Don't be an even greater ass than God made you, Leonard. We suppose dyslexia to be a functional disorder. Its presence is commonly detected in children—often very intelligent children—as soon as they're presented with their horn-book. That's known as the "developmental" form. We know now not to panic or fuss, and the condition can usually be persuaded to fade out. And it has always interested me. Thirty years back, if I remember, I told you I was going to look into it.'

'So you did. I do now recollect that too.'

'But there's also, you see, a much rarer form of the trouble. We call it "acquired", and I'm always on the look out for it.'

'It attacks adults?'

'Just so. And here, suddenly, it walked in on me in the person of the boss of this dump we're gorging ourselves at the expense of this evening. And what could be handier—downright nicer—than that? But now here's his underling almost certainly attacked as well. It's damned awkward. Suppose it spreads like billy-o.'

'Like mumps, you mean, or some such harmless thing?'

'If mumps comes at *you*, Leonard, you mayn't find it harmless. Celibate, aren't you? It may remind you of what you carry round with you, all the same.'

This was distinctly coarse even for Martin Brand, and for a moment it silenced me. And my host of the evening became aware as a consequence that he owed me a little chat. So I got nothing further out of Martin until we rose from High Table and went into common room for dessert. But I did have a quick murmur from him at the end of the evening, when we were collecting our discarded gowns preparatory to going our several ways.

'Of course, there are possibilities,' he said. 'Distinctly there are possibilities. It's occasionally a small bonus one gets when landed in a fix. Meanwhile, what's the betting that that praepositai understudy is in my consulting-room tomorrow morning? I'll put a quid on it. Or a bottle of claret. The dump allows that in its wager book.'

'Not on,' I said, and departed into the night.

Living, as I have explained, merely on the periphery of academic Oxford, I was far from surprised that for nearly a week I heard nothing more about the misfortune that had befallen the Provost of Judas, but I did on several occasions find myself reflecting on its extreme oddity. That a mature and distinguished scholar (as the man must surely be) should suddenly find himself, although retaining all his faculties in their full vigour, bereft of the earliest and most humble of his acquirements—to wit, the ability to read—was as bizarre as it must be profoundly disconcerting. I could well understand his retreating into unexplained seclusion until the disability should either pass or have to be admitted as dictating a total change in his manner of life. I even found myself wondering—and the wonderment was itself bizarre—whether he chanced to possess an informed knowledge of flowers and plants, and would thus be able to retreat upon such useful but decidedly unassuming toil as had marked the daily round of the now doubtless long-since deceased Howe. And the recovered image of Howe prompted another train of thought. Howe's manner of life had been mysterious in various small ways, and the need prudently to dissimulate his disability had inclined him to other concealments than the vital one. The Provost, if his affliction chose to settle in on him, might well decline upon a course of irrational obfuscations.

From this my speculations moved to Martin. Why had Martin been so promptly upset by the mere possibility that the Pro-Provost had, so to speak, climbed into the Provost's boat? When at length I did begin to hear the first stirring of general gossip about what had occurred, I noted that its tone of amusement about what had befallen the two men proceeded from the fact of its childishness; its suggestion of one kid catching the mumps or whatever from the kid at the next desk. And at this thought a fuller light came to me. It seemed that Martin Brand had made himself something of an authority on dyslexia, or at least was known to have been long interested in it. Did his prompt dismay as the Pro-Provost seemed unable to read what was on his ping-pong bat proceed from a sudden apprehension that the disability was *catching*; that there was, to put it crudely, a bug involved—whereas all his own theorizing hitherto had been in a different direction? Other hazy perceptions about Martin followed upon this one. As well as perturbation, I felt I had detected in him something like glee. What had he meant by saying that the situation held 'possibilities'? It came to me that the Galen Professor of Physike and Chirurgerie, for all his air of large self-confidence and heartiness of address, and perhaps in accord with that strong hint of hidden streaks or strains in him, had to be judged as essentially an unstable personality. I think I can honestly say that I recoiled from this notion almost as soon as it came to me. The man was generally liked; I had myself as a boy positively been fond of him; I had a genuine hope that he would wholly distinguish himself in his treatment of his new patient, the Provost of Judas.

It was not to be. The Provost did not return to that High Table. The Pro-Provost, too, was an absentee. A non-antiphonal, but equally elaborate grace was now being pronounced by an undergraduate.

But that was not all. Quite quickly, that was far from being all. It was a time of year at which the reading-rooms of the Bodleian Library ought to have been crowded with young men and women—with young persons, perhaps I ought to say—belatedly preparing themselves for the mild horrors of the Examination Schools. But those reading-rooms were now almost forsaken. Row upon row of untenanted desks testified to there being something badly wrong. Eventually, so sparse was the attendance that it took even a drastically depleted staff scarcely a couple of hours to fetch a required volume from the labyrinthine bowels of the institution. It was as if, after six hundred years, the Black Death were abroad once more in England.

But nobody, of course, died. And, at least among the young, few went into seclusion. Already at an ungodly morning hour—eleven o'clock say, or even ten—the semi-affluent and the affluent, scions of nobility and loitering heirs of city-directors, crowded the streets in their sports cars as they went off to fish, to shoot whatever the month allowed, to sport with the tangles of Neaera's hair in little temples, major follies, unfrequented recesses in stately homes and mere country seats. In the afternoons the river was more than commonly gay with punts, canoes, juvenile tuck-boxes, portable radios and record-players. Of an evening the poky restaurants were crowded, and money flowed the more freely because nobody could read the menu, or the prices against one bogus speciality or another. The student body—so wide and fair a congregation in its budding-time of health and hope and beauty—concluded without effort that books are a dull and endless strife, and that there was only blessing in the fact that all such—folios and quartos and duodecimos—had become a closed book to *them.* Only here or there a pale scholar or exhibitioner, sequacious of the ultimate glory constituted by a fellowship at All Souls, wandered, a lost soul, amid the throng of his liberated and unalphabetic contemporaries.

Inevitably, the thing rapidly became a national sensation. Nothing remotely to be thought of as an outbreak or epidemic of dyslexia had ever been heard of before. It was as unheard of as an outbreak or epidemic of two-headed calves. That it had occurred, of all places, in Oxford, a community relying for its livelihood and existence on reading and copying from books even more than on manufacturing motor-cars, added a piquancy—indeed, a weirdness—to the affair. And it was, at least for the present, an entirely localized phenomenon. Nowhere else in England, in all Great Britain, in the entire Western World was any change in the incidence of dyslexia reported. In Oxford itself, and with surprising speed, a whole new commercial activity sprang up. Working in respirators, and segregated as far as possible from the community at large, competent and unafflicted teams of hastily recruited persons toiled with tape-recorders to render audible what had been only legible hitherto: Stubbs's *Charters*, for instance, and Liddell and Scott's *Greek-English Lexicon.* An acute shortage of magnetic tape was made good by supplies flown in from Hong Kong; there was a hastily smothered scandal about a boom in what were called video nasties.

Amid all this, Martin Brand's position was peculiar and—after quite a short time—increasingly disagreeable. His connection with dyslexia, which was in fact clearly substantial, was much hyped by the press. He was described as the world's prime authority on a horrible and new-fangled scourge, and it was felt and declared that Oxford was fortunate in possessing on the spot the right man at the right time. But soon the attitude changed. Was it not at least a strange coincidence, it was asked, that the right man had been on the very spot on the world's surface upon which the hitherto unexampled calamity had occurred? Might there have been carelessness, criminal carelessness in some laboratory in which a quite minor and infrequent medical 'condition' was being studied? Had there been—it was a deadly word—a *leak*? The modern equivalent of Pandora's fatal box is a test-tube, and it is widely believed among the vulgar that a fractured test-tube may unloose unimagined pestilence over the planet. And whereas at the bottom of Pandora's box of evils Hope was found to linger, nothing of the kind has ever been discovered in a broken test-tube.

III

When I did run into Martin again it wasn't in the Hall or common room of his distinctly imposing college. It was in a pub: one of those small and inconspicuous pubs, presumably on the site of mere drinking shops in a former age, which tuck themselves away in Oxford even amid important shops and offices in high-rental areas. This one, I believe, was frequented in the main by college scouts and messengers, rather than by even the humblest academics. From across the street, I had suddenly become aware of Martin dodging into it, and for a moment I had the uncomfortable feeling that he had done so to avoid an encounter with me. But at once I saw that this was impossible, since I had turned out of a side street only in time to glimpse his disappearing profile and back. So I crossed over, and went in after him. There was a small and, at the time, empty bar, in which Martin was in the act of ordering a pint of bitter. I told myself that he wasn't looking well, and then saw that I was judging only by the irrelevancies of his being unshaven and rather carelessly dressed.

'Hullo, Martin,' I said cheerfully. 'I'll have the same—and on you.'

At this, and with a mere nod of recognition, Martin silently held up two fingers to the barman. I believe this was meant merely as a facetious suggestion of ungraciousness and resignation, and I record it only because of a curious and fugitive aberration it occasioned in me. I really did, that is to say, for a fraction of a second believe that what had stricken a large number of people in Oxford was not word blindness but mutism. Then—equally oddly and as if from a remote past—I seemed to hear Martin saying, 'a large number of people can be quite a small percentage of *everybody*'. This, in turn, put into my head something I wanted to know. But—in turn again—I went about attempting to satisfy this curiosity with a cautious obliqueness. It was a time, of course, at which we were all a good deal on edge.

'Did you ever,' I asked, 'read that thing about triffids?'

'The day of them? Yes, rather a good yarn.' Martin glanced at me suspiciously. 'So what?'

'The earth passes through the debris of a broken-up comet, or perhaps some nuclear missiles collide in orbit. As a result, a high proportion of the human race is instantly struck blind. But we're not told just how high. And I'm wondering about this little epidemic here in Oxford. Just what percentage of the population has it hit?'

'I don't know. I know nothing about it.'

'My dear Martin!' I was shocked that he should adopt so absurd an attitude.

'Well, then—I know as much as the next man.' Professor Brand had the grace to look slightly ashamed of himself. 'But just consider, Leonard. If you're blind, you can't move a dozen paces without manifesting the fact. But if it's just that you are suddenly unable to read, the conclusion need be apparent to nobody as long as you keep clear of print. And people are *ashamed* of being unable to read. Remember Howe. And they're ashamed of it even when it's a sudden physiological thing. Many keep quiet for as long as they can. I suppose the majority here in Oxford divulged the thing at once, and tried to have something done about it. The surgeries of the wretched G.Ps were crammed straight away, and there were queues at the hospitals. Up at the John Radcliffe the car-parks were full. Just think of that.' Martin was now speaking fluently and forcibly. 'But respectable statistics remain hard to collect. Moreover, there's nothing to say to people when they clamour. If you have no clear view of the damned aetiology of the thing, you're not likely to be too hot on prognosis. That's what I mean when I say I know nothing about it. And it's bloody awkward, believe you me. Why am I in this rotten little pot-house? Because here I'm unlikely to run into the inquisitive and pestering professional classes.'

'Meaning me. I apologize.'

'Oh, you! You're useful, Leonard. A harmless old crony, to whom I can blow off steam.'

'Then go on doing it. What's so awkward? Is it just that you are the top authority, at least in these provincial parts'—I scarcely know why I pitched this stupid barb at Martin—'who finds himself baffled and unable to come up with anything?'

'Well, not exactly.' Martin plainly felt that I had put this too steeply. 'I can *talk*, you know. I can even do a bit of literary talk—triffids and whatever. Do you remember *The Doctor's Dilemma*?'

'Bernard Shaw's play? Certainly I do.'

'The phagocytes, and all that. There's a doctor who knows how to boost their action, but it's fifty-fifty whether or not it's at an advantageous moment. The Duke of York comes into it.'

'I don't remember Shaw's saying anything about the Duke of York.'

'It's my own *façon de parler*. The noble Duke was sometimes going up the hill, and sometimes down. According as to whether the little buggers in the patient's body were going down or up—and to that there wasn't a clue—the doctor was going to cure him or kill him. At least that's my recollection of the nonsense in what's an uncommonly amusing play. My present position isn't exactly an analogous one. But it's not far off.'

'Another pint, Martin? It'll be on me.'

'Another pint then. I haven't been exactly idle, you know. In fact I've been working on this monstrously atypical outbreak of acquired dyslexia like mad. Probably exactly that. Like *mad*.'

'Well?'

'I'm pretty sure I could now *induce* the thing, even if I'm short on the wherefore and why. But I'm damned if I know how to *stop* it.'

We were both silent for a moment. If I didn't positively gape at this extraordinary assertion, I certainly ought to have. The barman, who may or may not have been attending to our conversation, produced those second pints.

'So I have to mind my Ps and Qs,' Martin presently went on. 'Otherwise, I might find myself locked up. But I don't mind telling *you* that some uncommonly odd ideas come into my head. For example, that a malign and supernal intelligence is at work. A Spirit Sinister or Spirit Ironic, as one of your poet-johnnies has it. Just consider where the pest has been directed to operate. In Oxford, I ask you! Where more noses are stuck into books per square mile than anywhere else on earth.'

'The irony is apparent,' I said. 'It has even come into my own dull head.' I don't think I said this in any very good temper. I had, of course, brought this conversation on myself by following Martin into the pub. So I was being ungenerous if I was now feeling him to be a bit of a bore.

'But where else would be more ironic still? Or rather—to be perfectly frank—more devastating? It's an intriguing speculation, wouldn't you say?'

I may well have gaped again at this. Certainly I wasn't yawning. In fact, the notion of Martin Brand as a bore abruptly faded. And this was less because of what he had said than because of how he had looked. It was as if the boy rather than the professor was suddenly before me, and the pint pot of beer ought to have been a bottle of ginger pop. The boy, it will be recalled, had long ago struck me as nursing a fondness—as I may now put it, having Bernard Shaw in mind—for upsetting apple-carts if they came his way.

At this point we parted, and I went about my proper business. I hadn't ventured to say to Martin that if Oxford is full of libraries and books, so is it full of laboratories and establishments for medical research, and that there were those rumours going round of a broken test-tube or the like for which he himself might eventually have to carry the can. He had probably thought up this one for himself. Anything of the kind was, surely, next to nonsense. Nevertheless, it was possible that some thought of it had prompted his odd remark that, failing due care, he might find himself locked up.

IV

As the term drew on, the academic community—and, I suppose, the citizenry as well—grew more and more on edge. The Provost of Judas had emerged from his seclusion, and dined three or four times a week in Hall, as his custom had been for many years. Any important guest was, of course, set down at his right hand, and for this person he would produce a decent minimum of conversation—as again his habit had for long been. His disability, alleviated in no degree, was cautiously respected by all—no servant venturing so much as to place before him the little typed card enumerating the men both dining at his table and proposing to take wine thereafter. And if he glanced down the long benches of undergraduates with more than common severity, it was probably because of an exacerbating circumstance unknown on the occasion, say, of the plague in Shakespeare's London. Nobody *pretended* to have the plague. But a good many undergraduates of the more than commonly idle sort were darkly suspected of feigning dyslexia, and of thereby freeing themselves from the more irksome aspects of the student life. Dyslectic dons could, of course, still listen to essays in the few instances in which pupils were available to read them. But it was useless for them to wake up thereafter and hurry off to the delights awaiting them in the Bodleian or elsewhere, since these repositories had become for them veritable *fontes signati*. More than commonly, learning was virtually at a standstill.

In such a strained society it was inevitable that irrational persuasions should begin to form. And they thus formed, most unfortunately, round the Galen Professor of Physike and Chirurgerie.

*

I have mentioned the conviction or suspicion—itself sufficiently grotesque—that our strange visitation had resulted from some culpable lack of care in a laboratory, and presumably in a laboratory under the control of Martin Brand, who was known to conduct research into dyslectic disorders. For this, which I may call the test-tube theory, there was, I imagine, no ponderable evidence at all, and it is therefore shocking enough that it should have gained even momentary credence within a learned community. But yet more shocking is what further came to blow around. The disaster, it was whispered, had by no means been inadvertent. Brand, who was known to speak scornfully of the university and its ways, had acted as deliberately as Aeolus when, at Juno's command, he struck with his trident and loosed the fury of the winds upon the Trojan voyagers to Latium. This elegant comparison (thought up by the Corpus Christi Professor of Latin Language and Literature) grossly flattered the squalid and demented act thus attributed to the wretched Martin Brand. And 'demented' became the operative word. There was born and propagated what may be called the theory of the mad scientist. And a scientist by no means just lately, and perhaps passingly, overtaken by madness. It was known to many of his intimates—the story ran—that Brand even in his infancy had planned diabolical operations against his fellow creatures. From his earliest days in medicine he had interested himself in dyslexia with just the present fiendish joke in view. And if that isn't madness, what is?

It would appear probable that it was precisely as a joke that this version of the matter began. But mere reiteration gained it credence or at least a kind of half-belief. I didn't, of course, even half-believe it myself. Yet I did believe that Martin's interest in the dyslectic state had been generated in an Oxfordshire garden long ago. But for that, he would have no particular interest in it now, and not have become the centre of disobliging speculations to which he might indeed react not in the most responsible or stable of ways. In this last persuasion I was to prove well in the target area.

*

I have known Cambridge men surprised to learn that their university city is actually a few miles nearer London than Oxford is. For Cambridge, much to its advantage, substantially keeps itself to itself; it is from Oxford that there is a constant stream of busybodying academic worthies. In my own earlier time there, many dons enjoyed every week what they called their 'London day'. For this they would don their 'London suit'; equip themselves further with a bowler hat, an umbrella and a brief-case; and travel, first-class return, to Paddington. Their pupils of the better sort, identical in turn-out but minus the brief-case, were frequently doing the same thing; and with these they would amiably and approvingly converse. Latterly, the *res angusta domi* has a good deal cut into this, so far as the rank and file of learning goes. But a new and smaller race has arisen of persons much more august than these: that upper crust even of the Oxford élite, heavies even among the Heads of Houses, whose wisdom is sought in the arcana of government. These go up to town to say a word in the Cabinet Office; to give the right nudge in the right Ministry at the right moment; even to stand up and deliver a deeply informed speech in the House of Lords. Returned to Oxford, they will occasionally murmur to an unassuming colleague in a corner some breath of what has been transpiring in the very councils of princes.

It was thus that we began to hear of the sinister metropolitan occasions of the Galen Professor of Physike and Chirurgerie.

Essaying only the sparest of narratives, I here pass over preliminaries: the whisperings at second-hand, the rumours of undetermined provenance. There came a morning upon which I was sitting in my little basement office in Wellington Square, endeavouring to sort out the affairs of a retired Fellow of Oriel College who was proposing to lecture on Restoration Comedy in the lesser universities of Uruguay, when the door opened and my boss stuck his head into the room. (I say 'my boss' to emphasize again my humble status in the city of dreaming spires.) It was seldom that he thus ventured half-underground. He was now in an unaccountably agitated condition.

'Burton,' he said with a tremor in his voice, 'there's somebody called to see you. It's Martell.'

'Martell?' I said. 'I don't know anybody . . .'

'Good God, man! *Charles* Martell. He's the P.M.'s p.s.' Maxton (which was my boss's name) might have been saying, 'He sitteth on the right hand of God the Father Almighty'. So I hope I looked impressed. In fact, I confess to *being* impressed. Nobody from the corridors of power had ever—so to speak—rung my bell before.

'You'd better show him in,' I said.

'I thought, perhaps, that in the circumstances, my own room . . .'

'Show him in, Maxton,' I said firmly. It wasn't, after all, Maxton that this emissary from on high asked for. And I suppose that already I had an inkling of what was cooking.

'Oh, very well.' Maxton disappeared, and moments later ushered in the great man.

'Mr Burton,' Maxton said, 'is a valued colleague. I must apologize for the accommodation, Sir Charles. Our budget, if I may venture to mention it . . .'

'How do you do?' Martell said to me, and briskly shook hands. 'Thank you,' he said to Maxton. So Maxton withdrew, and my visitor surveyed my cubby-hole with some care. 'Mr Burton,' he asked, 'can we by any chance be overheard?'

'Oh, yes—I expect so.' I said this in a cheerful and carefree way, having a hunch that I'd have to be treading warily, and judging that a little lightness of air might usefully suggest that I wasn't going to be trodden on. But, of course, the chap knew better than that. His manner was, in fact, extremely courteous. 'Then, perhaps,' he said, 'we might take a turn in the garden. It's familiar ground to me. A good many years ago, I had digs in Wellington Square.'

'I was in Holywell,' I said.

'Ah, yes. Convenient for you as a New College man.'

So Martell had done his homework—or, rather, had it done for him. We left the building. Wellington Square cannot have been any longer much like the place my visitor remembered from his undergraduate days. But he seemed well-pleased to talk as we perambulated in what remained of its secluded centre.

'Let me be clear at once,' he said. 'The Prime Minister is very concerned about this extraordinary outbreak in Oxford. He is anxious to be kept informed about it. And particularly about the incubation period.'

'My dear Sir Charles, why on earth should you come to me about that? It isn't remotely my sort of thing. But I have gathered—merely from reading it up in the last few days—that most authorities would regard talk about an incubation period as nonsense. Dyslexia, when it occurs in maturity, is regarded as the consequence of a small-scale cerebral disaster. If it happens, it happens bang off.'

'Would that be—or would it now continue to be—the opinion of Professor Brand?'

'I've no idea.'

'But the Professor is—is he not—among your intimate friends?'

'Nothing of the sort. We were at the same prep school, and now see each other from time to time. May I say that I consider it very extraordinary that you should wish to talk to me about him?'

'It is indeed extraordinary. But we are faced with an extraordinary situation. And not merely in Oxford, Mr Burton. In London as well. Or, to be more precise, in Whitehall, in the Houses of Parliament—and, indeed, in Downing Street. In Number 10, Mr Burton. Yes, positively in Number 10 itself.'

At least a breath of all this had already come to us in Oxford through the channels I have described. As a consequence, I was able to give some attention to the form, as well as to the substance, of what Sir Charles Martell had said. I judged him to have a nice sense of climax.

'So I appeal to you, Mr Burton. I appeal to you on the instruction of the Prime Minister himself. You say that your acquaintance with Professor Brand is comparatively slight. But at least it stretches far back. Is it in your memory that he nursed'—and Sir Charles paused to choose a phrase—'revolutionary predilections?'

'My dear sir—a boy at his private school!'

'But it is *most* important. We must uncover everything we can: mere hints though they may be. In your more recent chats with the Professor, has he ever let slip an interest in, even an admiration for, the principles of communism as they inform the governments of Eastern Europe?'

'Never.' I saw that things were getting serious. 'But go on,' I added. 'If I am to help you Sir Charles, I must be put in the picture.'

'I fear that might take me beyond my instructions.'

'Then, sir, we'd better call it a day.'

'Very well—but I rely upon your absolute discretion. And I ask you to imagine a Cabinet Meeting confronted with papers none of which those present is able to read.'

'It is certainly a remarkable thought.' I resolved to be a shade perky. 'But I don't know that it would matter very much.'

'The chain of command, sir! The flow of intelligence! Consider the convenient questions which back benchers are instructed to get up and put to Ministers. Of course they have to be written down for them. Good fellows, no doubt—but more likely than not to be of mediocre intelligence. One couldn't possibly trust them to do the job *viva voce*. And that is only one tiny instance of the mischief threatening us. The entire system of government would grind to a halt. We are, of course, making our contingency plans, but time would be required to bring them into effect. And in that fatal interval an enemy might strike. Lacking directives, our armed forces would be in chaos.' Martell paused briefly. 'The Dyslexia Factor,' he said solemnly, 'would be decisive. Our defeat would be certain from the start.'

'Dear me!' I said. I believe I was really alarmed by this sudden vision of paranoia in high places. 'Just how can poor Martin Brand affect so comprehensive a mischief?'

'By squirting it.'

'I beg your pardon!'

'The things are called aerosols. You kill flies with them. Or, for that matter, obtain the stuff you shave with. In a confined area such as Westminster, and granted the possibility of an imperceptible and odourless vapour. . . .'

'I can see, Sir Charles, why you want to know about an incubation period. But—even granted the theory that there is a bug, or virus, or whatever. . . .'

'The situation here in Oxford proves that, does it not? What you call cerebral disasters don't suddenly happen by the hundred.'

I saw that Martell had a point there, and I paused to consider.

'Even so,' I then said, 'have you any evidence whatever that this machination has been in Brand's head?'

'Conclusive evidence. Not only has he of late been coming constantly up to town, and cunningly insinuating himself into vital places. He has even been observed—and photographed!—gloating over the things.'

'The things, Sir Charles?'

'The canisters containing the deadly stuff. Alone in a first-class railway carriage, and believing himself safe from detection, he opened a haversack and counted over the deadly objects.'

I find it hard to believe that, at this point, I failed to tumble to the true—and sufficiently shocking—state of the case. But I am uncertain about this, and recall only that I at once asked two further questions.

'Am I to understand from all this, Sir Charles, that Professor Brand has occasioned widespread dismay and panic throughout the Government; that every Minister, and innumerable less exalted persons, are waiting apprehensively for dyslexia to descend upon them?'

'I would not express the matter in precisely those terms, Mr Burton. But in substance your conjecture is correct.'

'Then why on earth don't you arrest the man? He must be clean off his head.'

'Precisely so. We are apprehensive that, upon an unwary approach with the object of putting him under restraint, Brand might take some summary means of making away with himself. Taking with him the secret of the antidote.'

'If there is one.'

'The cure, the treatment—what you will. If the man can propagate the thing, he can certainly put an end to it.'

'It's an assumption,' I said—and didn't add that Martin had named this to me as exactly what he couldn't do. 'And I still don't know, Sir Charles, why you have come from town to tell me all this.'

'Because it is clear from our inquiries, Mr Burton, that you are in Professor Brand's confidence. We look to you to sound him out. Perhaps, if you judge it to be judicious, to hint to him that he has been unmasked.'

At this last word, something like melodrama appeared to hover over my colloquy with the Prime Minister's right-hand man. I felt I'd had enough of him.

'I'll do what I can,' I said. 'Have you come up to Oxford by car?'

'By train.'

'Then we'll go back to the office, Sir Charles, and I'll call a taxi to take you to the station.'

V

It seemed to me that the situation required a little thinking over. I decided to let a day pass, and then simply tell Martin, in careful detail, about my disconcerting interview with Sir Charles Martell. The sequel would be up to him.

But this failed to happen, and when I did again see Martin it was under changed circumstances. What took place began with my remembering, just after Martell had left me, that on that evening I happened again to have an invitation to dine in Judas. If Martin chanced to be dining too, I could, with a very little manoeuvring, covertly study him without having to join him and converse. Why I should have taken it into my head that this would be in any degree advantageous, I don't clearly know. There was a good deal of muddled thinking in Oxford by this time, and probably I had my share of it.

Standing, as before, while awaiting grace, I quickly saw that Martin wasn't in evidence. But the Provost was in his place at the head of High Table, as was the senior fellow facing him in the prescriptive fashion. The Provost, of course, knew that grace by heart, so his affliction was neither here nor there so far as the ritual performance went. The precise drill was this: the Provost would give a dignified nod to the head servant who managed things in Hall; the servant would give his bellow; the long rows of chattering undergraduates would fall silent; the Provost and senior fellow would fall to the business of alternately haranguing their *deus omnipotens, pater caelestis*. But a hitch—indeed, an unexampled impropriety—now manifested itself. At the bottom of the Hall a lounging young man, perched on the end of a table, was reading a newspaper—no doubt with some obscure notion of showing off to those of his companions who could have done nothing of the sort even had they wanted to. And the Provost observed it. He motioned to the butler standing behind him.

'Give that gentleman my compliments,' I heard him say, 'and require him to come up here at once, bringing his paper with him.' This was a sensation—but only a very minor sensation compared with what was to follow. The message was delivered, and the offender, amid a dead silence, walked up the length of the Hall and presented himself before the Provost. The Provost eyed him for a moment before speaking.

'Your name, sir?'

'Kilby, Mr Provost.'

'Mr Kilby, gentlemen do not engage themselves with the public prints when attending upon the common meal.'

'I'm very sorry, Mr Provost.' Kilby now clearly judged it proper to be oppressively correct.

'Hand me that paper.'

Kilby did as he was told. The Provost glanced at the thing, and his brow darkened. 'What is this?' he said. '"*Vicar's Love Nest in Vestry*". And "*My Joy Ride with Sex Maniac*". The gutter press! Mr Kilby, consider yourself admonished.'

'Thank you, Mr Provost.'

At this, Kilby received back his paper, and returned to his

place—in a silence that now had stupefaction added to it. There could be no doubt as to what had been demonstrated. *The Provost's word blindness had evaporated.*

And so, within a few days, had that of everybody else who had been visited. This held throughout the town—of scholars and citizens alike. At the railway station the time tables could be consulted; on the streets everybody could see where the buses were going to; the reading-rooms of the Bodleian were crowded again. Quite soon, as with an epidemic of influenza, the thing was forgotten about. But I did have a brief conversation with the Galen Professor of Physike and Chirurgerie.

'Explain,' I said.

'I've told you before,' Martin said. 'I know nothing about it. No more than the next man, I said. Don't you remember?'

'I remember your saying that you could start it, even if you couldn't stop it.'

'It was a lie,' Martin said comfortably. 'I had to cheer myself up, you know. The whole affair is nonsense, so far as anything known about dyslexia goes. And I'm not going to be the man who tries to make sense of it. Plenty of young chaps around to get going on that.'

'But, Martin, you don't deny that you played the fool with a pack of aerosols and whatever, and put the fear of God into the entire Establishment?'

'If a bunch of morons takes one for a mad scientist, why not give them a run for their money? I think I did pretty well.'

'Aren't you afraid they'll lock you up?'

'Not in the least. They'd only expose themselves as having been first-rate chumps, wouldn't they? No, no—they'll keep mum about it all. I'm all right, Jack.'

TWO STRINGS TO HIS BOW

I

GEOFFREY SIMKISS HAD believed for a good many years that he had come to terms with himself as a harmless little man. This wasn't a matter of the comfortable frankness that steals upon many in middle age. Simkiss was still quite young when the persuasion of his own near-nullibiety looked to have become a settled thing with him. Even so, it had been a little procrastinated by the fact of his having been appointed a professor at the startlingly early age of twenty-five. Premature promotion had arrived partly because he was intellectually precocious and rather clever as well; and partly because, at the critical moment, there had been nobody else around who had shared with him his interest in the early history of English lexicography. Within five years of his taking up his Chair he had become the sole authority in the field worth appealing to, but had also arrived at the perception that the subject was of limited interest not merely to the world at large, but to his own learned world as well. So he began to wonder how he could branch out from it.

Simkiss said 'branch out' to himself rather than 'break loose' because he was reluctant to contemplate positively quitting the academic profession. Even in slightly paranoid phases, when he believed (wholly inaccurately) that some of his colleagues had formed the habit of actually articulating the phrase 'harmless little man' by way of describing him, he still didn't want to quit university life. It was true that the pupils who gravitated to him were on the dull side, and that at those boards and committee-meetings at which his rank should have assured him of a respectable hearing, quite a number of people distinguishably switched off as soon as he opened his mouth. But on more relaxed occasions most of his colleagues chatted to him cordially enough, and without their glance too often straying to other parts of the room. He liked his midday meals in what was called 'Staff House', where a bustling woman knew to bring him a little carafe of wine along with his corned beef, and at which there was small-talk which he could sometimes positively brighten with an apt quotation or a suddenly remembered undergraduate joke. Moreover the pay wasn't bad, and he had twice got himself brief holidays abroad at the university's expense by discovering that there was to be a lexicographical conference in Bonn or Uppsala. So at first he thought of a little increasing his stature (which was the real problem) by what might be called cognate studies: adding, for example, early orthoepists (with whom he already had some familiarity) to the early dictionary wallahs, or venturing seriously into the tricky field of Finnish loan-words in Old High German. But these things meant much labour for somewhat exiguous rewards, prestige-wise regarded. He wouldn't exactly walk tall on the strength of them. It was because there was a streak of genuine ambition in him that he wanted so to walk.

So what about breaking loose after all—but in some fashion compatible with staying put? There was the comparatively new race of persons called 'TV dons'—commonly so named with a disparagement more than a little tinctured with envy. Given the necessary assiduity, might not the higher-class chat shows become open to him? But somehow he didn't much relish the idea of going home and a few evenings later viewing himself on the box—or even having so to view himself during the recording in a battery of screens ranged round the studio. Always a diffident man, Professor Simkiss was on far from easy terms with the shaving mirror in his bathroom, and still less with the long looking-glass that hung beside his bed. TV wasn't on.

Steam radio (a term he believed to be decidedly modish) was another matter. There, you offered the world nothing but your voice. Unfortunately he wasn't altogether sure about his voice—or (to put it crudely) his accent. The microphone, he knew, was an extraordinarily sensitive instrument, and there were certain vocables on which he wasn't reliable. He could say 'bun' and 'Hun' to himself half-a-dozen times, but when it came to 'one' he produced the noise you make when you speak of wan and emaciated faces, or something like that. There was nothing—he told himself—merely snobbish about this. It was simply that an orthoepist ought to know how to pronounce common English words.

So what other spare-time activities were open to professors—to professors of his own sort, without any scientific training to exploit? He knew that his colleague, the Professor of French, was the unobtrusive proprietor of a pie shop, and that the Professor of Egyptology was the master-mind behind his wife's flourishing travel agency. But he himself was both a vegetarian and unmarried, so there seemed to be no road that way. But other professors *wrote*. There was distinctly more promise there. In his earlier schooldays, and well before he had developed his philological aptitudes, some master had recorded in a report that he wrote with a natural grace. Why not again start writing with a natural grace? There might be real kudos in it. There might even be money as well.

But write *what*? At a first review of this problem it seemed to him that the most appropriate output for a professor of the Humanities would be of essays and things of that sort. Charles Lamb, Simkiss rather vaguely thought, and Edmund Gosse. Lamb hadn't, perhaps, done too well out of it, but Gosse had belle-lettered himself into the job of Librarian to the House of Lords: a position as excitingly exalted as it was soothingly secure. But on second thoughts here, Simkiss discovered there was a snag. Essays had distinctly gone out. Nobody wrote them any more, or at least nobody got them published. Of course the idea of reviving a whole literary kind had its intoxicating side. But Simkiss, who was essentially a modest man, decided he wasn't quite up to that.

Many professors wrote book-reviews. Some even succeeded in disguising as book-reviews what were in fact essays of that old-fashioned sort. In this trade, moreover—although it was comparatively small, and therefore probably rather hard to break into—there seemed to be considerable scope for various temperaments, and even *varying* temperaments. The same chap, that was to say, could be pretty well gushing one week and uncommonly acrid the next, even when the transition was effected before literary labours virtually indistinguishable the one from the other. But although this large scope was—such is the frailty of human nature—powerfully attractive, the fact remained that an uncomfortable whiff of Grub Street attached to the whole activity. And its emoluments, probably, weren't all that.

Professor Simkiss then thought of *novels*!

His Department consisted of himself and an Assistant Lecturer called Hugh Lockton. Lockton was, of course, quite young—yet still not all that younger than himself. He was rather wary of Lockton, who he suspected was one of those given to speaking of him as a harmless little man. They were on familiar terms with each other, nevertheless, and as Lockton's casual conversation revealed him as a novel-reader in quite a big way, Simkiss thought he might, at least obliquely, sound him out on the matter.

'Hugh,' he asked, 'would you say that a good many academics nowadays occasionally turn novelist?'

'Lord, yes! Bevies of them. Campus fiction, mostly. It's all the poor devils know about. How long have I been in this bloody hole? Just over three years. The world forgetting, by the world forgot: that's me. And the same with them.'

'I haven't looked into it myself.' For a moment Simkiss hesitated to continue. He disliked the manner in which the absurd American misuse of the word 'campus' had rapidly acclimatized itself in England. He rather disliked 'this bloody hole'. It was true that their university wasn't Oxbridge. But it was a fairly old-established 'civic' institution, and not one of the mushroom affairs sprouted in the 1960s. However, he resolved to continue. 'It seems to me,' he said, 'that what you call "campus" fiction would be best written by people *outside* the universities. A matter of the spectator seeing most of the game. Think of Trollope, Hugh. As what you might call ecclesiastical fiction his Barsetshire novels have no rival. But he never lived in a cathedral close.'

'My dear Geoffrey, Trollope was the next thing to a *great* novelist—meaning, you know, a *major* novelist. We're talking—

are we not?—of failed or discouraged scholars splashing about in the shallows of the thing.'

Simkiss didn't like this possibly proleptic vision either. So he said, rather stiffly, that he hadn't happened to expose himself to much of the splashing. But, supposing he wanted a dip, where should he begin? He could, he supposed, get some of the things from the public library.

Lockton was silent for a moment. He was all too plainly wondering what this was about. Perhaps he guessed—for when he spoke it was with the ghost of a derisive grin.

'The only decent campus novels are detective stories. And I mean "decent" both ways on.' Lockton paused again on this cryptic remark. 'You can see how it is: a lot of fairly cerebral characters more or less in a sealed room. Staircases and quads and all that. I haven't read many, but I remember rather a good one. Set in Oxford and called *An Oxford Tragedy*. It's by a don who was a very considerable swell in quite different fields of endeavour—but with this itch to scribble. Name of Masterman.'

'I must get hold of it,' Simkiss said dishonestly. He had no intention of writing whodunits. 'But there must be a good many serious novels in a university setting. Indeed, I remember one of them. It was called *The Masters*. It struck me as rather good.'

'Did it?'

Hugh Lockton, who was getting even more bored by his chief than usual, contrived to utter these two monsyllables to so rude an effect that Professor Simkiss closed the conversation, and went away to do some thinking.

He saw almost at once that—particularly at the outset of a writing career—one has to draw on one's own experience if anything in the least convincing and verisimilar is to emerge. It wasn't, of course, a hard-and-fast rule. Bits and pieces could always be done on the strength of second-hand experience. For example, he had an elder brother, who had also been a very clever boy at school, and who was now a civil servant moderately high up in Meat, Poultry and Eggs. Although he didn't see this brother very often, he was fairly sure that he could get him pretty faithfully into a book. But Meat, Poultry and Eggs don't take one very far if one's aim as a novelist is, say, the achieving of a comprehensive picture of Man in Society such as Tolstoy and similar masters of the novelist's craft provide.

So Simkiss realized that he must do some serious thinking about what might be called his *world*. What was its circumference? In what particular areas was he aware of it *in depth*? Where on his map were there to be located the regions of his particularly vivid awareness of things? He asked himself quite a number of questions of this sort—scurrying on to the next because there always seemed to be a bit of a hold-up in coping with the last. He asked himself, for instance, about women, since women figured quite prominently in a great many novels. He couldn't tax himself with being utterly incurious about women. He did wonder about them from time to time. His dreams, and one or two other things, told him he wasn't what his students nowadays called a poof. But when he *thought* about women a large blankness took possession of his mind. Soberly, he acknowledged that here lay a considerable disability. He could, of course, go to work on women here and now. He could get them up—much as he could get up a new language. But, as with languages, women would take time. Much reading would have to be done. He might even have to go to parties.

Checking an impulse to move on to something else, he continued to worry at the woman business. His mother had died when he was quite young. He hadn't any sisters. His grammar school had been a boys-only affair—and he had entered its junior department at seven and left from the sixth form at eighteen. Oxford in his time had equally been a boys-only experience, with girls-only colleges as the sole receptacles for females that the place provided. Now, of course, he had students of both sexes (or 'genders', as they were beginning to say), but he didn't see much of any of them except in lecture-rooms. All in all, he hadn't had a chance. Pass on to something else.

Passing on, and circling round and round, Professor Simkiss was almost driven to the conclusion that his entire life so far had been devoid of any pronounced experiences whatever. It had always been his belief that he was the possessor of a capacious memory. But, now scrutinized, the capaciousness seemed to be rather exclusively a matter of abundant information on issues of a learned and indeed recondite sort. He could recall the occasion of many of these acquisitions with surprising clarity. He could see in detail, for instance, the notched and inky school desk at which, with commendable speed, he had mastered the Greek alphabet. But what of *boyhood*—its sorrows and its joys, its companionships, games, hobbies, and so forth? From all those long years he couldn't securely recall a single damned thing entitled to be called an event. It was all most discouraging. *A novelist?*—he seemed to hear the mocking voice of young Hugh Lockton saying—*Don't make me laugh.*

But Geoffrey Simkiss possessed pertinacity. Without it, how could he have coped with the birth of lexicography, or the decay and death of Old High German? He sat down and wrote a novel.

In this first novel he was thoroughtly drastic with himself. There were *no* female characters. The action never strayed beyond the curtilage (*scilicet* campus) of a redbrick university. There was a fairly complicated plot, turning on a dispute between colleagues about who had first discovered the importance of a manuscript found lurking in the library. This didn't, of course, lead to anything of the 'whodunit' sort. Nobody was found knifed in the refectory. On the other hand, there was no shirking of unsavoury matters when they turned up. One of the professors was found to be secretly using a photocopying machine in contravention, if not of the law, yet plainly of the ethics of copyright. The Vice-Chancellor was sometimes more than a little tipsy after attending official dinners of the University Council. So there was no nervous avoidance of the seamy side of things.

The novel was reviewed in several papers, and all these reviews had at least something agreeable to say about it. Not knowing that there is a convention about treating first novels in this way, Professor Simkiss was a good deal encouraged. And then he was actually interviewed! The interview, it was true, was conducted by a woman on behalf of a local weekly paper, so it wasn't exactly the kind of affair that later gets collected into a book. The young woman struck Simkiss as vaguely familiar, so it was possible that a few years earlier she had sometimes appeared in his lecture room. He found this conjecture slightly disconcerting—as he also found the fact that she had brought along a tape-recorder and planted it in front of him. She appeared, moreover, not to be a very experienced interviewer, and she had also brought along a set of prepared questions on a scratch-pad.

'Professor Simkiss,' she asked, 'by whom do you regard yourself as having been most influenced?'

Simkiss felt rather blank before this, and his impulse was to say 'Nobody at all', since that, although odd, seemed to him to be true. But he reflected that a claim to absolute originality might be regarded by the tape-recorder as on the arrogant side. 'Dostoyevsky', he said—and was promptly appalled. The absurd name had simply bobbed up in his head, and out he had come with it. Dimly, he knew that the tape-recorder had got him on the run. But he fought back. 'Dostoyevsky, decidedly,' he said with weight.

'And Dickens?'

'Dickens?' It didn't seem to Simkiss that the young woman had any business to chuck novelists at his head in this random way. 'Why Dickens?'

'I think Dostoyevsky is known to have been influenced by Dickens.'

'Perfectly true.' Simkiss had never, indeed, come across this fact, if fact it was, but he spoke with the authority of a man who is conscious of having ground to recover. 'We, too, have our pedigrees, you know. Chains of command! We trace each other everywhere in the snow.' Simkiss fell silent on these disjointed utterances—shocked, this time, by a sense of making gibberish out of other men's aphorisms, and tumbling the result into the woman's horrid little machine. In the ensuing silence the machine could be heard softly turning the tape on its pivots, hungry for more. And the nightmarish occasion did continue for some time—remorselessly recorded, Simkiss felt, for all eternity. It was only when the machine clicked to a stop that the young woman packed up her scratch pad and called it a day.

'Our photographer,' she said, 'will come this afternoon. He would like you to wear your mortar-board and gown.'

'I will do nothing of the kind, madam.' For the first time, Professor Simkiss allowed himself to become quite cross. He had made a fool of himself, he felt, and might just as appropriately appear with a bauble and bells. 'And I'm not sure that I want to be photographed. But I suppose I must put up with it.'

'It's not like the dentist,' the young woman said cheerfully, and dropped the tape-recorder into a shopping-bag. Then she switched abruptly from professional to human curiosity. 'I say!' she said. 'Whatever put it into your head to write a novel?'

Simkiss knew what the reply to this ought to be. It was something like, 'I had an overpowering sense of possessing a unique vision of life which I must communicate to others'. But he was by nature an honest man, and honesty triumphed. 'God knows,' he said. 'I don't.'

The young woman received this without surprise, and at the door she asked a final question.

'And are you going to write another one?'

'Certainly,' Professor Simkiss said. 'And I'm going to start at once.'

In addition to being an honest man, Geoffrey Simkiss was (as has been mentioned) a pertinacious man as well.

His second novel turned out to be very like his first. At its centre was a contentious issue of a familiar academic sort. Which of two deserving scholars, each long-established within the university in which the story was set, should be promoted to a vacant Chair? The committee charged with sending a nomination to Council took its duty very seriously; it met, adjourned, met again on a weekly basis throughout an entire university term. There was much temperate debate, and many cogent arguments in favour of one candidate or the other were deployed, weighed, answered. Amid the domestic sanctities of the senior professors, too, discussion between intimate colleagues often went on far into the night. Simkiss reported it all.

Where the second novel *didn't* follow the first was into that territory which the tyro Simkiss had vaguely thought of as affording a slightly risky light relief. Nobody now ran a profitable little side-line in cut-price photocopied cram-books. The Vice-Chancellor was strictly sober. Simkiss had been puzzled and rather hurt that—with the exception of Hugh Lockton—none of his colleagues had ever referred to the first novel, although many of them must at least have known of its existence. This, Simkiss had concluded, might well be because they disapproved of its admitting, even in a passing fashion, what could be regarded as a *louche* element. So Novel Number Two was very pure indeed.

But still nobody uttered a word about it! This was the more vexatious in that Simkiss would have been particularly grateful for a little private commendation, since public commendation was in singularly short supply. About the same number of reviews appeared as before, and it was more often than not the same reviewers who provided them. But what had been 'brilliant' in the first book turned out to be 'conscientious' when found in the second; and 'conscientious' itself appeared in the appraisals a good deal less frequently than 'pedestrian'. Simkiss, who knew that the two books were at least much of a muchness, was puzzled and disheartened by this. Then he noticed that a substantial proportion of the reviewers were female. So that was it! *Varium et mutabile semper femina.* Or (Simkiss reflected) as Richard Stanyhurst had translated it:

> *a windfane changabil huf puffe*
> *Always is a woomman.*

Lockton had provided him at the outset with a short reading-list in campus fiction, beginning—perhaps a shade whimsically—with *Tom Brown at Oxford* and *Zuleika Dobson.* But Simkiss had refrained from reading either these early masterpieces or later works by near contemporaries of his own. He judged—reasonably enough—that this abstention distinguished him as a writer of independent mind. When he had fully established himself, he felt, it would be quite amusing to discover how he stood in relation to these fellow-labourers in the academic vineyard. So disregarding, indeed, was he even of reviews and advertisements of such things, so innocent of quite celebrated names, that he almost set out on a small examining job at another provincial university in ignorance of what he was to find there. Fortunately, he was obliged to mention his expedition to Lockton.

'Hugh,' he had said, 'you'll have to hold the fort next Thursday and Friday. I have to cope with a thesis at Nesfield, and I'd better spend the night in the place.' Nesfield, although also a university city, was a manufacturing town in a state of pervasive decay dating from Mahatma Gandhi's persuading his countrymen that they could do their own spinning on their own doorsteps. Even the university, although barely twenty years old, was distinguishably coming out in sympathetic cracks and flakings. Simkiss and his colleagues thought poorly of it.

'A D.Phil. thesis?' Lockton asked.

'I believe they call it a Ph.D. But that sort of thing. Extremely dreary reading.'

'And your fellow-examiner there?'

'Probably extremely dreary too. Name of Henfrey. Professor Gabriel Henfrey. I can't say I've ever heard of him.'

'Gabriel Henfrey? Good Lord! Geoffrey, haven't you done any of that reading I recommended to you?'

'I can't say I have.'

'Not even Henfrey's *Going Up*? My dear chap, it's the campus novel of the year.'

'Is it, indeed?' It was natural that Professor Simkiss should find this information startling. '*Going Up*, you say? Is it about freshmen arriving at a university? The phrase is pretentious if used other than with reference to Oxford or Cambridge.'

'So it is. But Henfrey's novel isn't exactly about that. You'd better get hold of it, and read it on the train.'

'I'll do nothing of the kind.' Simkiss felt that this was perhaps rather a churlish remark. 'I'll have to have—well, what you might call another go at the thesis. It's about Dains's *Orthoepia Anglicana.* Published in 1640, you know. And never looked at, probably, since Roesler and Brotanek edited it in Halle in 1908.'

'Probably not. But mayn't it be awkward if this Henfrey proves to be an enthusiastic fan of yours, and you have to confess you'd never even heard of *his* stuff?'

'It would no doubt be an occasion for the exercise of some address,' Simkiss said with asperity. 'Of course the man is giving me lunch before the candidate turns up for his *viva*, and we may have some general chat. But more probably we'll be trying to work out what we can ask the chap.'

'You just set the candidate talking, don't you?'

'It must be admitted, Hugh, that you know your stuff.' Simkiss chuckled with restored good humour. 'He'll quote everything he's said in his Introduction, and then repeat it because it's what he's said in his Conclusion. And we shake hands with him, and explain he'll get his result in six or seven weeks. Then we hand him back our copies of his whacking great thesis, and as he has brought a third whacking great copy into the *viva* with him, he will withdraw gratefully, but decidedly like a beast of burden.'

Professor Simkiss laughed happily as he said this. It was just the sort of vivacity with which he lightened his serious pictures of academic life.

Professor Simkiss saw at once that Professor Henfrey was a harmless little man. There was absolutely no vice in him, and not much voice either. He spoke in a muted fashion which overpoweringly suggested that he was apologizing for speaking at all. It was impossible to imagine that he could make himself heard even to four or five students in a seminar. But at the same time there was something feebly pompous about him. His conversation at lunch, so far as Simkiss could make out, was exclusively shop-talk of a learned sort, and he kept on referring to his and his guest's common concern as their 'discipline'. This was, no doubt, correct enough in a formal way, but it struck

Simkiss as pedantic and slightly absurd. It was astonishing, perhaps it was instructive, that so mild and milky-watery a creature should be a successful novelist.

But the subsequent oral examination, which the two professors conducted alone with their candidate in a semi-basement chamber, revealed Gabriel Henfrey in a different and rather surprising light. He was still barely audible, and for most of the time his gaze remained lowered in a diffident way upon the bulky typescript before him. Nevertheless, he could only be described as a ferocious examiner. And minutiae were very much his thing. An ectopic footnote, even an otiose comma, plainly made his blood boil; and for nearly an hour he drew attention to such things remorselessly and page upon page. The candidate, a large-limbed and clumsy man with close-cropped ginger hair, stood up well when scorched beneath this hard, dry heat of scholarship, and Simkiss began to feel himself distinctly on the poor chap's side. His own approach to the thesis was much more general, and he could sense that Henfrey disapproved of it. The situation was uncomfortable, even if not wholly unfamiliar, and he found himself nervously prolonging his own part in the affair just by way of postponing what he knew was going to be a row when the candidate and his burden of learned lumber had been bustled from the room.

'Riddled with inaccuracies,' Henfrey said as soon as this had happened. 'Riddled with inaccuracies from start to finish. It won't do at all.' He said this in a low, husky, and almost underdog way which Simkiss found extremely irritating. But there could be no doubt that the man meant what he said, or that he was other than deeply entrenched in his prejudices.

'Certainly carelessness here and there,' Simkiss suggested. 'Faults in expression, and some positive errors and contradictions. But, after all, it's a whacking great thing. And I don't feel that actual inaccuracy is all that prominent.'

So a long argument began. It is quite probable that Henfrey's stringent attitude was the right one, and that Simkiss's was tinged with a cynical indulgence censurable in a scholar. Of theses and dissertations of the kind before them now, it was his habitual if commonly unspoken view that the poor devils concocting them were going to have a living to earn, and if they sought to be 'D' something rather than merely 'M' something or 'B' something—well, why not? The ginger-haired man would be neither more nor less effective as a teacher in some dismal institution of further education whether as Doctor or Master or Bachelor. Moreover on the present occasion, whether rightly or wrongly, Simkiss was genuinely convinced that the thing was good enough for the desired stamp to be put on it, and he turned as obdurate as his colleague. Finally, he produced the awful threat of sending in an independent report. At this, as he expected, Professor Henfrey gave in. So Ginger (as Simkiss had come to think of him) received his degree.

Although satisfied at having got his way, Simkiss felt the entire incident to have been vexatious and undignifed, and it left him decidedly out of love with Nesfield. He had been a fool to come near the place, and he decided to remain in it no longer than need be. Abandoning his plan for a leisured dinner and a night in a hotel therefore, he made his way to the railway station to find an early train. As it happened, he had no more than ten minutes to wait, so he went over to the bookstall and bought an evening paper. Then he noticed that the bookstall actually ran to a few books: paperbacks for the most part, but a few in hardback as well. Among these latter there was a small pile of identical volumes, and above them a hand-written notice saying 'By a Local Author'. The book—needless to say—was called *Going Up*, and was by Gabriel Henfrey. Professor Simkiss bought it at once, and carried it with him to the train. A journey of a couple of hours lay ahead of him, and in that time he'd skim the thing through. Hugh Lockton had advised him to read it on the outward trip. Now, and having become acquainted with its author, he'd give it a go on the return. It was sure to be pretty dim. It might well be very dim indeed.

II

'I don't understand it. I don't understand it at all!'

It was the following morning, and Professor Simkiss had burst in some agitation into his Assistant's room. Lockton was standing in front of his little gas stove, toasting his calves when he probably wanted to toast his bottom, and three or four students were sitting glumly round a small table with open notebooks before them. The study of literature was in some sense going forward—but now came abruptly to a halt. Everybody stared at the intruder, astonished and gratified to see that the dim little man on whom at least an uncomfortable chunk of their destinies depended was in some sort of obscure distress.

'I think we'll call it a day,' Lockton said easily, and accompanied the words with a dismissive wave of the hand. 'The Professor has urgent business with me. Keep at it, and I'll see you all next week.' He waited until the young people had scurried from the room, and then turned to his chief. 'So what?' he said.

'Hugh, I suppose you've read those books you gave me a list of?'

'Certainly I have—and they're only *la crème de la crème*. Have you come asking for more?'

'You've read *this* one?' Ignoring Lockton's absurd query, Simkiss tossed *Going Up* on the table. 'The wretched Henfrey's novel?'

'Of course I have. It's quite amusing in its way.'

'Hugh, let me be plain with you. I gravely doubt whether reading such a lubricious composure—let alone judging it amusing—can be regarded as other than morally reprehensible.'

'Good Lord! But you've read it yourself?'

'Certainly. I read it on the train, coming back from Nesfield yesterday evening.'

'So at any time you could have tossed it out of the window?'

'I felt a certain obligation to pursue it to the end. The man is, in a sense, a colleague. In *two* senses a colleague. He holds a Chair of sorts in a university of sorts, and—and he is a fellow-novelist as well. But the saturnalian violence of the thing——'

'Saturnalian exuberance.'

'Do not quibble, Hugh. It *confounds* me. A little mouse of a man—although a pedantic mouse too——'

'Henfrey is just like—is like that? I suppose that when one is in the know about him, then, it adds a little to the piquancy.'

'Piquancy! The thing is, from cover to cover, a libel on an honourable profession. Philological conferences as a mere cloak for—for drunken chambering! For whore-hunting, Hugh! For a luxuriance in esoteric postures that would disgrace Aretino!'

'It has gone down very well. Let me show you, Geoffrey.' Lockton picked up *Going Up* and turned to the verso of the title-page. 'Just look. "Reprinted three times", and only within as many months of publication. And it has won a prize, you know. The Pumblechook Prize for a satiric novel. And I'm told that the translation rights have been sold all over the world. The Japanese version is out already. And it's sure to be pirated in Russia.'

Given this information, Professor Simkiss found himself silenced for perceptible seconds. He didn't at all know why. That the lewd book had been a success was neither here nor there—except, indeed, that it spoke of the general depravity of the times.

'But, Hugh,' he then said, 'consider the entire tone of the thing. It represents us collectively—dons, or whatever we are trying to be called—as given to a certain amount of shoddy intriguing and scrounging round in pursuit of promotion and casual emoluments. But in the main it depicts us as puppets in a mere sexual phantasmagoria.'

'Just that. Henfrey's book, and all the others more or less like it, aren't meant to be taken *au pied de la lettre*.' Hugh Lockton had a weakness for interlarding his conversation with phrases culled from the *Concise Oxford French Dictionary*. 'Think of your old pal Charles Lamb on Restoration Comedy. "A fiction, a dream, the passing pageant of an evening". And so forth. "Altogether a speculative scene of things". And, as I've said, amusing in its way.'

'Well, yes—but——'

'No call to behave like a wowser about it.'

'Like a what, Hugh?'

'Aussie slang, Geoffrey. A spoil-sport type.'

'I certainly don't want to be that.' Simkiss, although he was by no means as yet acknowledging the fact to himself, was finding something obscurely seductive in his junior colleague's attitude.

'Honestly now, Geoffrey. Didn't you get a laugh or two out of *Going Up*? Isn't it a damned sight less outright dull than that Cambridge thing you were talking about?'

'Cambridge thing?'

'*The Masters*, wasn't it?'

'Well, yes—but——'

'And with quite as large a whack of our unredeemed human nature?'

'I suppose that may be true.'

'But it could be bettered, couldn't it? By someone with a much larger talent as a writer than this Henfrey chap.'

'No doubt whatever about that,' Simkiss said.

Thus—as in some mediaeval morality—did Concupiscence, tempted by the distant trumpet of False Fame—overcome True Perceiving. Geoffrey Simkiss's third book had tremendous success. A panel of persons prominent in literature placed it at once among the Fifteen Great Novels of the Century. Reviewers called it savage, hilarious, unsparing, riotous, one in the eye for Petronius, minutely faithful to academic life, a bawdy extravaganza, dispassionate, owning a masterly power of telling understatement, a lashing flail from cover to cover, and the best thing of its kind since Alexander Pope's *Dunciad*. Then an organization called the League for Moral Purity in the Home sought to have it suppressed, and this just turned a final and delicate scale. Film rights were negotiated for a sum which, although undisclosed, was understood to be very large indeed.

All this was, in fact, a little hard upon Professor Simkiss. If he wasn't really a harmless little man neither was he (as some enthusiasts averred) a figure such as hadn't been seen in Europe since the death of Voltaire. He was still reluctant to cut out of university life, and he rubbed along with his colleagues and students much as before. As before—meaning the period of his first two novels—nobody except Hugh Lockton ever said a word about his writing. Even when the top photographers of the day came down from London and focused him amid the university's sham cloisters or in front of a blackboard scrawled with Anglo-Saxon remarks, people seemed unprompted to comment. Once, actuated by honest mischief, he invited Professor Henfrey to come over and examine with him. But Henfrey had nothing to say either about his own now somewhat eclipsed novels or about what might have been called Simkiss's Second Manner.

Professor Simkiss set about his fourth book. He had to, since he had signed a contract for it and received a substantial advance. Perhaps he started in on it too soon, for almost from the first he felt himself subject to what he believed economists called the law of diminishing returns. He had to work a little more broadly—coarsely, even—to achieve his designed effects. And this, in turn, he conceivably a little overdid. He was conscious that the novel, when published, was received with a shade of reserve. Of course the book was funny, the reviewers said, but some of its diversions were a little on the scabrous side. One critic, addicted to a German dictionary much as Lockton was to a French one, used the adjective *gemein*. All this naturally made Simkiss somewhat uneasy.

Then one day he went into Staff House to lunch. He sat down at a long table with, on one side, a man he scarcely knew, but who had once told him, mournfully, that he worked on potatoes all the time. On his other side was a vacant chair—and almost immediately one of the bustling women came forward and tipped it up against the table. Simkiss didn't make much of this. If one had arranged to talk over something with a colleague during the meal, and had arrived before him, one sometimes did this oneself.

A couple of minutes later, the Vice-Chancellor came in. He didn't often lunch in Staff House; in fact he did so only on becoming conscious that it was time to be a little affable in a general way. Now the Vice-Chancellor looked amiably round the room, and his glance fell, seemingly quite casually, on this reserved seat. He strolled up, pulled it out, and sat down.

He glanced at the neighbour thus provided for him with an air of slight surprise.

'My dear Simkiss,' he said, 'I don't often have this pleasure. Quite some time, indeed, since we ran into one another. Yes, *indeed*. I hope you're well?'

'Thank you, yes, V.C.' Without yet at all knowing why, Geoffrey Simkiss had to acknowledge to himself a distinct sense of apprehension.

'Department okay? Young Burton pulling his weight?'

'Lockton. I have no criticism of him at all. I sometimes feel—quite unreasonably about so young a man—that as a scholar he is surprisingly unacquainted with one or two obvious sources. Nothing of great consequence, you understand.'

'Ah, yes.' The Vice-Chancellor pretended no further interest in Hugh Lockton, but continued to converse cordially on one topic or another. Later in the meal he had a good deal to say to the university's Registrar, who was sitting immediately opposite him at the narrow table, and he turned back to Simkiss only at the same time as he made a gesture of polite refusal to a woman proposing to provide him with a hunk of suet pudding.

'I must just mention,' he said, 'the pleasure I have received from your new novel. Quite delightful,my dear fellow! Such seeming facility, to mention only its least arresting quality. It's hard to imagine how you can think of it all.'

'As a matter of fact, V.C., a good deal of effort is involved.'

'Effort after something new, I suppose. You may be described as having bided your time, as it were.'

'Bided my time?' It was a shade suspiciously that Simkiss repeated the phrase.

'I mean that you have made your contribution rather late in the development of the genre. Which accounts, conceivably, for one's slight sense of a fellow scraping the dirty bottom of the barrel.' The Vice-Chancellor got to his feet. 'I can spare a few minutes for coffee upstairs. There are several people with whom I should like to have a short chat. So, my dear Simkiss, good day to you!'

And the Vice-Chancellor, with a friendly nod here and there, departed from the room.

Scraping the dirty bottom of the barrel. . . . No hostile reviewer, willing alike to wound and to strike home, could quite equal the precise venom of that. Or so Professor Simkiss, perhaps in his sudden and deep perturbation exaggerating a little, told himself as he walked blindly round and round the dismal suburb in the centre of which the university lay. Some of his thoughts were entirely extravagant. He wondered whether, perhaps, the Vice-Chancellor had really been reading a book by the man Henfrey, and had got his authors muddled. He decided that Hugh Lockton had been as an Evil Angel to him, and he resolved to have him sacked. But—such is the disciplined clarity of the academic mind—such persuasions and fantasies didn't last long. Returning to his Department, and entering his room, he was already murmuring to himself several relevant apophthegms in a learned tongue. *Magna est veritas et praevalebit.* (Or was it *prevalet*, which was surely stronger and better?) *Ne sutor ultra crepidam*: prowling his bookshelves, Professor Simkiss saw that as comprising the nub of the matter. Yes, indeed: *let not the cobbler go beyond his last.* Suddenly, resolutely, with all passion spent, Geoffrey Simkiss put out a hand and took down a book. Its date was 1568, and its title *De Recta et Emendata Linguae Anglicae Scriptione Dialogus.* He hadn't been into it for quite some time, but he recalled thinking that, carefully studied, it could be made the occasion for a substantial contribution to a learned journal. He'd have a go at that.

NAPIER INTO FFINCH

'AN EXTRAORDINARY THING,' Mrs Danbury said to her husband as he came in from walking the dogs. 'The Napiers have changed their name, and have sent round a kind of circular to let everybody know. There it is on the hall table. See for yourself. And such a silly name, too.'

Colonel Danbury picked up the square of pasteboard.

'It does seem a shade odd,' he said.

'Whereas "Napier" means something.'

'Well, yes. There have been plenty of distinguished Napiers. Eminent soldiers and sailors galore—and with the man who invented logarithms thrown in. But the original associations of the name are not all that grand. It's the kind of name that is taken from a fellow's job. And originally French, I think. It merely means the man who looks after the table linen.'

Since leaving the army, Colonel Danbury had devoted a good deal of time to picking up information in one casually elected field or another, and had even amused his friends by gaining a degree from the Open University. Mrs Danbury was not wholly in sympathy with these activities, and the fact showed itself now.

'No doubt everything can be traced back to Noah's Ark,' she said. 'But whatever the occupation of the first Napier, the name doesn't sound simply silly, like this one. "Dicky-bird" would be no more ridiculous. And those two little *effs*. It's like a stammer.'

'Perhaps so, my dear. ffinch does look a trifle out-of-the-way. But I seem to have come across something about it somewhere. Just let me think.' And Colonel Danbury briefly thought—rather to the effect of a computer when it declares itself to be 'searching'. 'I have it!' he then declared. 'It goes back to mediaeval chappies in monasteries and places. Working on manuscripts in their scriptoriums or cells. They often indicated a capital letter by using two little ones. ffinch must originally have gained currency after some such fashion. It's pedantic, you may say, rather than pretentious. A mere typographical oddity. But it looks as if somebody has written it into his will.'

'You mean that the unfortunate Napiers have been constrained to change their name to ffinch because it has been made a condition of their coming into property?'

'Almost certainly that kind of thing, I'd say. Old families do tend to get quirky about such matters.'

'I never heard, Charles, of an old family of the name of ffinch.'

'Fair enough. But the ffinches may have had nothing notable about them for centuries except substantial wealth. Sometimes, you know, the change required is merely an affair of adding one name to another, so that you get that double-barrelled effect—or even three or four names on a string. I was at school with a boy called Cave-Browne-Cave. Old families there, all right. But we used to call him Home-Sweet-Home. Bad form, of course, making a joke of a fellow's name. But boys will be boys—or even louts at times.'

'But here,' Mrs Danbury said, 'it's a matter of people being required to *change* their name—and to something that looks extremely foolish.'

'Just that, almost without a doubt. Probably they haven't much relished it, but have decided the game is worth the candle.'

'Property will be involved?' Mrs Danbury's interest sharpened as she returned to this question.

'Quite a dollop, at a guess. It would take a pretty penny to make *me* go about as a ffinch.' Charles Danbury paused to laugh robustly at this notion. 'But no doubt every man has his price, as the adage tells us.'

'But doesn't the law have something to say about such ridiculous goings on?'

'I think not. There's nothing against the public interest in making such a stipulation in a will. If the chap affected wants to do things in a formal way, he makes the change by something called deed-poll. But if he just wants to call himself something else as a matter of mere whim, there's nothing to prevent him from doing it on the nail. Or so I've rather gathered.'

'It seems to me, Charles, an awkward kind of thing, any way on. But perhaps the modern habit of being on Christian-name terms with almost everybody may make it less so. Just how widely, I wonder, have the Napiers sent round those little chits? To the entire county for a start, I suppose. And to the parsons and doctors and dentists and people like that, no doubt. But what about the cottagers, and the man and his wife in the pub? The Napiers have them all to that annual bun-fight in the park, and so must be considered as among their acquaintance. But "ffinch" will be a great puzzle to all those worthy people.' Mrs Danbury paused, and then went off on another tack. 'Everybody knows that the Napiers, in spite of their broad acres and so on, are dreadfully impoverished.'

'Just like ourselves,' Colonel Danbury said, and again laughed heartily. His own poverty was a topic on which he liked to discourse at large—and particularly when regaling friends to a substantial dinner. He was a wretchedly premature half-pay man, he would declare, with nothing to look forward to but an Old Age Pension in the middle distance.

'So perhaps'—Mrs Danbury went on—'the wealth of the ffinches has come as a godsend to the Napiers, whether they like it or not.'

'I'm sure I hope so, my dear—but it may be rather a ticklish affair at some deep level of the mind.' Colonel Danbury was again 'searching'. 'In primitive societies there can be an obscure magic about one's name, the anthropologists say. You don't willingly grant your enemies access to it, because the knowledge would give them some power over you. Curious idea.'

'I wonder just how much is involved?' Mrs Danbury was uninterested in the anthropologists. 'Is there any way of finding out?'

'You might ring up the Hall, I suppose, remembering to ask for Mrs ffinch, and when Bella comes to the phone put the question to her straight.'

'I hope that it will at least be enough to provide handsomely for their daughter.' Mrs Danbury must have regarded her husband's humorous suggestion as so feeble that it should be ignored. 'Particularly as poor Jane Napier is, unhappily, so unattractive a young woman. So far as looks go, that is. She may be clever, or good at croquet, or something of that sort. We seldom see much of her.'

'Jane ffinch, you ought to call her. I rather think the change of name will henceforth apply to the whole of the family. But I agree that Jane's chance of a suitable husband will be much enhanced if there's a substantial sum to settle on her. How like we still are to those people in what's-his-name's novels.' Yet once again, Colonel Danbury had set his private computer to work. 'Trollope,' he said. 'Anthony Trollope.'

'Bother Trollope! And do you know, Charles? I'm rather wondering whether we ought at once to tell Nicholas about this new state of affairs at the Hall.' Nicholas was the Danburys' only son.

'Why ever should we do that?'

'Nicholas and Jane both live in London, although I think it's without meeting very often. But there are always parties. It might embarrass both the young people if Nicholas were led up to Jane and told he was being introduced to Miss ffinch.'

'I don't quite see the force of that.' Colonel Danbury cast a glance of what was something like suspicion at his wife. 'The two of them know each other well enough. Here at home they've played tennis and so forth from time to time. They'd simply tell their hostess or whoever that they knew one another already. And then the girl would explain to the boy why she was now Jane ffinch. No embarrassment about it at all.'

'I don't know why you should go on calling Nicholas a boy, Charles. He's a grown man, surely, although not a very successful one so far. Has it ever occurred to you that it's high time he got married?'

'Married! In our day, Dorothy, it was still felt that a young man ought not to propose marriage to a young woman until it was clear that he could provide an establishment for her. Very Victorian, and all that. But sound sense in it, all the same.'

'Jane, just like Nicholas, is an only child. And we are agreed, I think, that the Napiers have made this idiotic change of name only because doing so brings them some very large fortune.'

'I don't know that we are agreed on that "very large". But let that be. The fact is that you see yourself in the role of a successfully scheming mama. You want to give Nicholas a head start in what may be called the ffinch stakes. Jane is due to come into money in a big way sooner or later. When that becomes generally known there will be no end of young men after her. And Nicholas, who hasn't earned a penny for several years so far as we know, must get ahead of them. He pretty well has a duty that way. What's-his-name again.'

'Trollope.'

'Yes, damn it, Trollope.' It was almost in a bad temper that Colonel Danbury acknowledged this. But he regained equanimity at once. 'Very well. Write and tell the boy. I've nothing against my own son—unless it's his reluctance to have his hair cut. And success will come to him rapidly when it does come. I've seen it often enough on my own cabbage-patch. You run into an impudent subaltern, and the next day there he is on the General Staff. Whether he has married an heiress or not.'

On this firm note Colonel Danbury—as he frequently did—gave way to his wife, and Nicholas was informed by letter of the new state of affairs at Hinton Hall. Hinton Hall was quite an imposing country house, and Napiers had lived in it for several generations, buying a little more land from time to time, and so coming to enjoy a kind of squirarchal status. This added to the oddity of their suddenly becoming ffinches. There was soon general agreement in the neighbourhood with the Danburys' persuasion that some very considerable fortune must have been involved.

Nicholas Danbury had been a reliable if not particularly studious schoolboy, who had gained coveted prestige by playing for the First Eleven in three successive summer terms. But on going up to Cambridge he had stopped playing cricket, and, perhaps as a consequence, had taken a surprisingly good degree. This properly gratified his father—who in his heart, however, would have preferred to see him scoring a century in the Varsity Match. Then Nicholas did something wholly unexpected and rather upsetting. He announced that he was 'going to knock around for a bit'; made sure that his father would until further notice pay a monthly sum into his bank; and thereafter simply disappeared. Over a period of several years his parents received no more than occasional picture-postcards: some of them from Paris and others from New York. He then turned up again, and announced that he had become a painter.

Mrs Danbury hadn't at all known what to make of this, but was thankful to have her son restored to her on any terms. The colonel, although no very pronounced devotee of the arts, stood up for his son. Nicholas, he declared, was entitled to go his own way—and his own way proved to include a few longish periods in the family home: this, perhaps, at times when he was particularly hard up. (It was thus that he came to play tennis, or otherwise disport himself, with Jane Napier and other of the local girls.)

Nicholas never painted during these fallow weeks, so that his parents had to make occasional journeys to London in order to glimpse the fruits of his labour. They were perplexing fruits. Whenever a human figure appeared in one of their son's paintings it was either floating horizontally in space, like somebody in an elaborate conjuring trick, or else it was simply upside down. If Nicholas occasionally sold a picture he kept dark about it, and his parents came to believe that nothing of the sort ever happened. But again his father refused to admit himself as altogether disheartened by this lack of commercial success.

'Remember,' he asked his wife, 'that affair I took on Art and National Culture? There was a bit in it about a johnny called Cézanne. French, of course. He made no impact at all on the picture market for quite some years, but he kept at it. He said that he reckoned to be the Primitive of a New Movement—and that was exactly how it turned out. You couldn't buy a sizeable Cézanne now without something like a million pounds in your pocket. Perhaps Nicholas is the Primitive of a New Movement too.'

'I expect he had money,' Mrs Danbury said. 'That Cézanne, I mean.'

'I rather think he did inherit considerable wealth from his father.'

'So there you are! Nicholas certainly won't do that.'

With this Colonel Danbury had to agree, although he didn't at all relish having to do so. He liked to speak of himself as 'keeping up with things', but in fact there were numerous territories over which his mind moved only in a thoroughly old-fashioned way. It was grievous to him that an only son should have no expectation of at least some modest inheritance one day turning up on him.

'This Jane Napier or ffinch,' he said to his wife, 'seems a clean-run girl enough. But I really know very little about her. What does she do with herself in London?'

'I understand she's the secretary to some magnate in a big business way, and thoroughly efficient at her job.'

'A nine to five sort of person then. With a typewriter and so on.'

'I believe it's rather more elastic than that, so far as the hours go. And that she's something of a power behind the scenes.'

'I don't much care for the sound of that, somehow. One has to think of compatibility, you know. On the one hand you have Nicholas, who's an artist and good luck to him—but a bit vague about other things. And on the other you have a career-oriented girl who we think is due to come into considerable wealth in her own right. It all seems to me rather the wrong way round.' Colonel Danbury paused for a moment before this somewhat elusive point. 'You might get them to fall in love with each other, and all that. But they'd almost certainly develop a life-style that made Nicholas dependent on his wife pretty well for every five-pound note. For you couldn't reasonably expect the ffinches to make a settlement on our son, could you? It would be a completely topsy-turvy kind of thing. Rather like the way Nicholas is fond of painting people.'

Producing this stroke of wit put Colonel Danbury in good humour, and he was content to rest on it. But he decided on some man-to-man chat with Nicholas when next the boy came home. His wife, he knew, would go to work circuitously and by dint of veiled hints and petty manoeuvres; she had said 'Bother!' (a thoroughly Trollopeian ejaculation) when he had mentioned Trollope, but it would be exactly in the manner of Trollope's scheming mamas that she would attempt to nudge her son into what she had decided would be an advantageous marriage. The colonel himself had concluded after some reflection that it was indeed high time that Nicholas, despite his impecuniosity, got married, and he would advance the proposition to his son in a general way. But if Jane Napier's name bobbed up as a result, he would not fail to say a word about the domestic pitfalls into which a young man might precipitate himself as a consequence of marrying into money. Of one thing he could be reasonably sure. A few years before, he had accidentally come upon his son kissing and tumbling a village girl in a barn. Withdrawing unobserved, he had experienced great relief at this solid evidence that there was nothing out of the way about the lad. Nicholas, within hail of thirty as he now was, could safely be presumed to possess some first-hand knowledge of the satisfactions to be obtained by getting between the sheets with a woman. That could be tacitly taken for granted in the man-to-man talk.

'That was an odd piece of gossip you sent me about the Napiers,' Nicholas Danbury said to his mother. Nicholas had come home at short notice for what he called a long week-end, and he produced this remark entirely casually as he sat down to his first dinner at the parental board.

'Not exactly *gossip*, Nicholas. I don't think that when I write to you I bore you by recounting anything like mere idle talk.' As she said this, Mrs Danbury reflected that she had got rather out of the way of writing to her son at all frequently—perhaps because, when she did write, her letter seldom prompted a reply. And she was conscious that, in the letter she had written only a few days before, she had wrapped up her vital news about the Napiers in a certain amount of local chit-chat by way of what might be called camouflage. It wouldn't do, she had felt, too hastily to disclose what she had in mind for Nicholas. 'There's a certain mystery about the thing which it might amuse you to set about solving,' she went on. 'It's your father's guess that the Napiers have had to change their name in order to receive some rather large family bequest. But that's pure speculation—and, of course, we can't ourselves very well broach the subject with the senior Napiers. Rupert and Bella Napier may explain the matter in their own good time. But it has occurred to us that you might receive an explanation from Jane.'

'From Jane,' Nicholas repeated blankly. 'Oh, Jane! Jane Jane tall as a crane.'

'Whatever does that mean?'

'It means nothing at all. It's in a poem. Yes, I suppose Jane Napier must know what this change of names is about. ffinch, did you say? I'll ask her if I happen to run into her. I do—from time to time.'

'Clean-run girl,' Colonel Danbury said, almost automatically. The expression, obscurely connected with salmon fishing, was a favourite with him and highly commendatory. 'Jane hasn't, I suppose, changed her name off her own bat?'

'By getting married, you mean? I don't at all know, but I think it's unlikely. I saw her at a party the other day, and she didn't seem to be hugging any lord and master. Come to think of it, she had that positively *virgo intacta* look. A ffinch, you might say, not yet fully fledged.'

Colonel Danbury frowned, as if judging his son's recourse to Latin distinctly indelicate. And when he spoke again it was with a certain inconsequence.

'Looks aren't everything,' he said. 'Everything about a girl, I mean. If a girl is decently bred, and healthy and with a head on her shoulders and isn't exactly a beggar. . . .' The colonel broke off, as if the thread of his discourse had eluded him. 'She may be plain,' he began again, 'but, if you ask me. . . .'

'Jane Napier *plain*?' Nicholas interrupted. 'Don't make me laugh! The head on that girl's shoulders is pure Modigliani, and to be admired in silence by anybody with an eye in *his* head and a scrap of artistic training.'

'Then wouldn't you like to see more of her?' Nicholas's mother asked—quite unconscious of having achieved an odd ambiguity. 'She may be spending this week-end with her parents. Shall I ring up and find out?'

'Capital plan,' Colonel Danbury said. 'It wouldn't quite do to ask Rupert and Bella to a meal—not so soon after receiving their chit about the ffinch business. It would look intrusive, you know. A kind of fishing for information on what's behind the thing. But Jane's another matter. If she happens to be there, we'll have her over to dinner. No, not dinner. Lunch—so that the two young people can take a walk through the woods afterwards.'

But at this final suggestion Nicholas Danbury stood up so abruptly that his chair clattered to the floor behind him.

'In heaven's name,' he asked, 'just what is all this in aid of? You seem both to have taken leave of your senses. A walk through the woods? Just what's cooking?'

'If you sit down again, I'll tell you.' It was clear to Colonel Danbury that he must take charge of the situation, and speak frankly. 'It's a matter of the family kitty, my dear boy. There's not going to be much in it for you later on, I'm afraid. No security to look forward to like Cézanne.'

'Cézanne?' Not unnaturally, Nicholas Danbury repeated the name in sheer bewilderment. But he did sit down.

'And here's this girl—whether Napier or ffinch—the only child of parents who are almost certainly coming into something in a very substantial way. And so we have thought—your mother and I—that if you and this pleasant, clean-run——'

'For heaven's sake, Daddy, stop talking nonsense. It's—it's the most indelicate ploy I ever heard of.' Nicholas was again on his feet, and this time he was making for the door. 'I can't listen to a word of it, or say anything at all. Not until later on, and when taking you, Daddy, for a walk through the woods.'

And Nicholas Danbury departed with half his dinner uneaten.

The walk took place on the following morning. It began in silence, but after a couple of hundred yards Nicholas spoke.

'You see,' he said, 'I couldn't say anything much yesterday evening—not with Mummy there. But now'—Nicholas glanced swiftly but appraisingly at his father—'being, as you are, a man of the world, and all that, we can speak frankly to one another.'

'Certainly we ought to have whatever it is out between us. Of course complete frankness is decidedly the proper thing.' The colonel was much flattered that he should be judged by his son to be a man of the world. 'So out with it. Is it true that you are married already, and have for some reason kept the thing secret from us? A wench you'd got in trouble, eh? And have done the right thing by her. And if there's a child likely to be in the picture——'

'Do be quiet and listen to me, Daddy. It's nothing like that at all.'

'I'm very glad to hear it.' Colonel Danbury realized that he had spoken out of a persuasion that artists as a body roam the land, seducing maidens, and leaving a trail of illegitimate progeny behind them.

'It's been nothing of that kind.' For a brief space Nicholas appeared to allow himself to be amused. 'If it had, I think I could have confessed to it before Mummy at dinner last night. But it's something so intimate and—and carnal, that I just couldn't do it. But with you it's different.' Nicholas again glanced appraisingly at his father as he drove this point home. 'Jane and I became lovers quite some time ago.'

'Just what do you mean: became lovers?'

'Made love. But it just didn't do. We are close friends still, mark you. We do concerts and theatres together. All that kind of thing. But in bed it turned out to be bloody well no go at all.'

'But, Nicholas, it often happens that a first time——' This was the voice of experience speaking. The colonel, although naturally much distressed, almost managed to feel pleased with himself.

'I'm not talking about a first time. I'm talking about half a dozen times. I just didn't turn Jane on—nor she me, except in the most demeaning and functional manner. She had to tell me that she got no more feeling from it—from *that*, I mean, than if I'd been a gent who was going to leave a ten-pound note on the mantel-shelf. Funny, wasn't it? As soon as our clothes were off it was just bloody and bleakly n. g. And here's you and my mother thinking to cook up an entirely blissful marriage of convenience. Danbury marries ffinch, and everybody applauds and throws confetti and old shoes. Jesus Christ!'

'Nicholas, has it been the same with any other woman or women?' Colonel Danbury felt that he had to keep an end up.

'Not a bit. Of course I've had near-tarts—and one or two wives of other men, for that matter—with whom it was a shade squalid in the recollection. But I really believe that Jane and I *wanted* to love one another. There was something like that.' For a moment Nicholas seemed lost in thoughts totally obscure and even frightening. 'But this blighted planet is like that, isn't it? Delighting in nasty surprises. Yet Jane and I haven't quite given in to it. As I've said, we continue to see each other, and to enjoy that. But on the bedroom side of things we've both agreed to—well, to undertake other commitments.' Nicholas was silent for some minutes as the walk went on.

'Do you think,' he then asked, 'that you can explain all this to my mother?'

Colonel Danbury, in his turn, was silent for some minutes. And then he spoke with decision.

'Certainly not. It wouldn't do at all. With the womenfolk, you know, a little prevarication is required at times, and is quite in order. But it won't be plain sailing. You and I must put our heads together, my dear boy.'

SWEETS FROM A STRANGER

IF I WERE a professional writer I could probably make a short story—a modishly sinister short story—out of the mere episode (as it was) that I propose to recount here. Alternatively, and were I a historian, I could so frame it that it showed like a footnote to a phase of Scottish social history. Indeed, with something like this latter I see I had better begin.

In the final quarter of the eighteenth century, then, the superior classes in Edinburgh began building themselves a New Town. Hitherto they had lived in a more or less mediaeval city to the south of the Nor' Loch, higgledy-piggledy with the poorest of the poor, but fortified, no doubt, by an equal contiguity with such elements of the Scottish aristocracy as maintained a town house in the capital. In many instances the migrating *haute bourgeoisie*, while losing the contiguity, very consciously maintained shades and degrees of kinship with this augustly territorial stratum of Scottish society. This is a very Scottish thing.

When they had built their New Town the *haute bourgeoisie* fairly quickly decided that it ought to contain a New School to which to send their sons. Hitherto these sons, had, of course, also lived higgledy-piggledy with the sons of the humble and unwashed, and if they sorted themselves out from time to time it was to engage in 'bickers' with their less fortunate fellows. A 'bicker' was a gang-fight likely to lead to a good deal in the way of bruises and gashes occasioned by clubs and stones. I don't think that as a boy I had so much as heard of these broils, which had evaporated from the popular memory. Perhaps I first read of them in Lockhart's *Life* of Walter Scott.

Hitherto, again, gentle and simple had gone to school together. The Edinburgh High School had for centuries held an unchallenged place at the head of Scottish scholastic education. Everybody went there, down to the future Sir Walter himself. But it was tough and rough. Moreover, it was situated, not in the commanding position it enjoys today, but in what was now thought of simply as the slums. The persons planning or plotting for a new and exclusive school made much of the inconvenience—and worse—likely to be encountered by their sons in their daily going to and fro this ancient place of education. So the new school was built, and Sir Walter was wheeled in to make an opening speech.

I have written all this by way of highlighting the essentially insulating class-structure of society which intensified itself (I believe) throughout the nineteenth century—perhaps even more in England than in Scotland— and into which were born those who, like myself, passed their infancy before the First World War.

In due course I was despatched to the preparatory department of the 'new' school—now, indeed, within sight of its centenary. I don't think there were many—if, indeed, any—boarders in the prep, and I certainly cannot yet have come to think of the boarding houses as strongholds of mysterious wickedness. I knew nothing about wickedness, except as something that frequently turned up in the Bible. And from the Bible when produced I had early formed the covert habit of removing my mind and thinking of Tom Thumb. My mother, however, must have been very aware of the Devil, and that he was among us, having great wrath. For on one of the first days of my returning from school she suddenly gripped my arm in its bright new scarlet blazer and uttered a strange question with yet stranger intensity.

'Donald, you *do* know that there is such a thing as *vice* in this world?'

Here again was something on which my mind was entirely blank. But I had discovered by this time how best to cope with sudden incomprehensibilities from grown-ups, and I hastened to assure my mother that there was nothing I didn't know about vice. This, perhaps a shade oddly, at once relaxed whatever anxiety had been harbouring in her consciousness. But what can it have been? The question puzzles me to this day. What scope can she have imagined the Devil as having for manoeuvre in what was called Class 1 B? In 1 B we weren't exactly toddlers any longer, but our ages must have averaged out at about eight. It wasn't as if my mother bore any sort of habitually prurient mind. In her own way, she belonged to an Age of Innocence as completely as I did myself.

And here is another type of insulation operative in this environment in which I grew up. There was a kind of tacit censorship upon any explicit ventilation of the seamier side of things. So far as I can remember, almost nothing of the sort even got into our newspapers. The existence of mere poverty was, of course, acknowledged; and although I don't recall hearing that distinction between the 'poor' and the 'good poor' which many Victorian philanthropists had managed to be aware of, there was, I believe, a vague and diffused feeling that a condition of indigence was in itself reprehensible, and that contact with it should, if unobtrusively, be avoided. Cousins of my own age in Moray in the distant North, some of them of families a good deal grander than ours, I had observed on holidays playing freely with the farm labourers' children. Nothing of the sort with us. All Edinburgh boys other than our own schoolfellows we referred to as keelies, which is Scots for street-arabs. And for weeks on end, any member of the poor with whom I ever conversed was in uniform, like tram conductors or our own maids—the latter being distinctively dressed in crisp aprons and caps, and being rather carefully 'well-spoken' as well. It would only be when a tramp (and there were a good many tramps around) came to the door and had to be found a 'piece' that I held the slightest commerce with these virtual non-persons.

I appear rather to be harping on all this. But it serves in part to explain the element of shock in my small adventure.

'Adventure', I see, is the wrong word. 'Experience' might be better. But, whatever it was, it was something startlingly new to me, and I am surprised to find that I cannot with any certainty put a date to it. In formal studies of the psychology of childhood, precise dating must, I imagine, be vital—and by 'dating' I of course mean determining and stating the age in years and months at which one or another significant act of behaviour has been produced. Even when children crop up in works of fiction one rather wants to know just how old they are supposed to be. When a novelist hedges over this, ignoring the point, or passing over it unemphatically and with no reiteration, I am left with the sense of him as not confident that he knows quite what happens to children when. This may be unjust, and I am far from being an authority on literary matters. (In point of fact I work as a solicitor—of the kind called in Scotland, perhaps a shade mysteriously, Writers to the Signet.)

But I return to my episode (another possible word for the thing) and its dubious chronology. And here I am at least given a hint by my bicycle. The bicycle comes into the story because one of the first explanations I afforded myself of what was happening was simply that there was a design to purloin it. And it was my *second* bicycle. I am very certain of that. My first bicycle had been an unassuming and locally manufactured affair. My second was resplendent: rigid, rapid, and reliable. And my father, since he was a leading surgeon, distinctly well-off, and amiably disposed to spoil his family, may well have given it to me on my tenth birthday. Further than this on the point, I can't go.

I was already not very fond of games, and I wasn't much of a reader either, although I have become something of one since. In summer I collected butterflies, and in winter postage stamps: clearly I wasn't an imaginative boy. I may also have been slightly isolated from my schoolfellows—this because we lived not in the New Town strictly regarded (the 'windy parallelograms', as somebody or other has called those august Georgian squares and oblongs) but in a large and somewhat retired house on its western fringe. This controlled the route I took home on my bicycle. If my journey was straight from the school itself I was companioned for part of the way up the ascent that led eventually to Princes Street. But if it was from our playing-fields, which lay at some remove from the main buildings and boarding-houses, I was on my own from the start, and quite early on there was one very steep incline which could be negotiated only by dismounting and pushing the Raleigh uphill.

In Edinburgh many people live in tenements. Elsewhere,

these might be called apartment blocks, or flats, or even mansions. But here they distinguishably exhibit something of their ancestry in the dwellings of the Old Town. Four or five storeys high, and with their ground floor occasionally turned into shops, they may extend the full length of a street as an uninterrupted terrace, with at regular intervals common staircases, stony and often smelly as well, giving access to small dwelling-places on either hand. Occasionally, however, these dwelling-places turn out to be, through some mysterious agency, more commodious than one would expect, and to be inhabited by persons distinctly of more consequence than their neighbours, and who don't at all seem to mind the often exhausting, grimy, and malodorous approach to their hall door. There is in this—as I say—some shadow of ancient times, when, on what has come to be called the 'Royal Mile', men powerful in the land were contented to live up just such a staircase, among neighbours who were at the best of the mechanic class.

Here and there around the city and its environs are oddly sited small examples of this sort of thing. It is as if volcanic eruption had tossed these bits and pieces high into the clouds, and then landed them at random, topside up but sadly in disrepair, in one unexpected place or another. There was a particularly good example on my left hand as I shoved my bicycle up that hill, and I believe that for some time I hadn't liked the look of it. But just what the look was, I can no longer say. The old woman and her gesture are etched on my brain, but the decrepit and—surely—half-abandoned building (demolished many years ago) largely eludes me. I have a vague picture of three storeys, the uppermost having windows broken for the most part and with rags of curtains blowing through. And I see the frontage rising not straight from the pavement, as was commonly so with tenements, but beyond a small patch of garden thick with thistle and nettle. The old woman as she makes that gesture is knee-high among this—which means that she has advanced a foot or two from the open door of the building.

She had beckoned me. She was not only old, but haggard and

dirty and bedraggled and dressed in what I thought of as rags as well. I was instantly horrified and frightened: of that I am certain. But the situation lasted only for a moment. I had shoved on the handlebars with a will, and the thing was behind me.

By the time I arrived home—and it was nearly all a breezy coasting once I reached the top of the hill—I knew I was going to be mum about that weird soliciting. Provisionally, I had decided that the old woman was a witch. I knew about witches not through fairy-stories or the like, but as a matter of family tradition. My maternal grandfather, having retired from the Indian Civil Service, had occupied himself in farming some scraps of land rented from a kinsman on high ground about midway between the small Scottish towns of Nairn and Forres. Much of the surrounding countryside is now patched with large plantations, collectively dignified with the title of Darnaway Forest. At a former time it may well have been heath—and blasted heath at that. Certainly from the upper windows of my grandfather's house one could remark a ruin, perhaps a couple of miles away, traditionally known as Darnaway Castle, and not far from this a small tump called Macbeth's Hillock. My mother, stretching (or contracting) things a little, would assert that it was on her father's ground that the new Thane of Cawdor encountered the Weird Sisters. It was almost as if we had witches in the family.

I knew that witches went in for that mysterious 'wickedness', and it must have been this that put it in my head that the old woman beckoning from her doorway was proposing to lure me from my bicycle (perhaps with the offer of a poke of jujubes) in order that it should instantly be carried off by a confederate. This persuasion remained with me as I hurried away, curiously shaken.

The incident repeated itself two afternoons later, and again I ignored that disturbing summons. But this time there was a new element in the situation—or, rather, there was something new obscurely surfacing in myself. And now I hesitate, since here are fugitive sensations fished up after more than fifty years. Am I dramatizing them if I suggest that a kind of dark excitement was getting hold of me? Certainly I no longer felt that it would be my bicycle that might be at risk if I obeyed that beckoning finger—the very gesture (my later self imagines) with which Goethe's Mephistopheles utters to Faust his final dire command: *Her zu mir!* The temptation—for it certainly now had that dimension—was alive in me. Prudent teachers, apprehensive parents are aware of such dark possibilities when they counsel children never to accept sweets from strangers. Still, I once more got safely home.

Some days went by, and again there was a 'practice'. (It was the term in which we played rugger.) As I 'changed' after the game and knotted my football-boots round my neck and wheeled out my bicycle, I knew that I ought to take the longer route home. But I didn't.

And there, yet again, she was: the filthy old hag—and not a soul else in sight. This time, however, she not only beckoned to me. She called out as well. In a cracked, wheedling voice she called out from before that shabby doorway:

'Maister, sweet wee maister, will ye no come ben?'

Donald, you do *know that there is such a thing as* vice *in this world?*

My mother's former words may, or may not, have been in my ears. I can't in the least tell. But I think I almost felt I knew, despite my innocence, what the reader (who isn't innocent) feels he knows: that some small, squalid, yet essentially evil thing confronted me were I to take a single forward step. But I took it. I wanted to *know*. Perhaps it was just that.

Here I must return for a moment to the theme of that insulated society within which I was growing up. I had heard my father speak of something he called 'the submerged tenth', and of an outrageous person named Lloyd George, who had made some minatory reference to 'the masses far down below'. But I had never glimpsed the inside of even a normal working-class dwelling, let alone of a slum interior of any sort. Occasionally I had been sent with a message to our jobbing gardener, and delivered it on the doorstep of what could be termed, I suppose, his hovel. But conscious that this could afford me a direct view of what must be its only living-room, I would keep my eyes as I spoke firmly directed on my own shoes. If at a pantomime or a play there was a scene set in what purported to be a cottage room, it would in fact be something like thirty feet from back to front and side to side. Television, which now renders the most nicely brought up children comfortably familiar with squalor in confined spaces and jostlings before a kitchen sink, still lay in the future. And now three forward steps had taken me into a totally alien world.

In front of me was a dusty stone staircase, protected by wooden banisters and a handrail of which only fragments remained. On my right was a door roughly boarded up—perhaps to discourage homeless persons from seeking shelter for the night in whatever small and abandoned dwelling-spaces lay beyond. On my left, but open, was the door of the still-beckoning old woman's own domain. Retreat remained perfectly possible to me, but I was as incapable of turning back as a mouse lured into a trap by a whiff of cheese. The room I thus found myself in wasn't, in fact, minute, but appeared so because everywhere encumbered with the forlorn detritus of utterly disordered living. It seemed that wherever I looked there was some broken or tattered object that ought to have been thrown away: a rusty mangle, pans without handles and pots without lids, piles of rags. The least battered piece of furniture was a bed, but even this was propped up at one corner on a wooden box. There was a horsehair mattress on it, with a triangular tear in its soiled covering so that the stuff showed through, and with a couple of tumbled blankets at its foot. I had never seen a bed on which it was impossible to imagine sheets, and as I looked at this one I suddenly felt very sick. Managing to avert my gaze, I saw that the room had a single window, facing the road and kerb on which my bicycle was presumably still leaning. Before the window was a chair, which seemed somehow to be perched on wheels. And on the chair sat a boy of about my own age.

For a moment I thought him much older, and then I saw that this appearance resulted from his features' being pinched and drawn. I saw, too, that he was awkwardly slumped in his chair, so that his body in its almost ragged clothing showed like a partly emptied sack. And he was powerless to right or relieve this posture in any way. I had heard of paralysis. This was it.

The old woman had taken me by the arm, as if to lead me, all-reluctant, up to the invalid. But now, seeing his discomfort, she let go. Almost, she had forgotten me.

'Jamie, ween,' she said as she hurried to him, 'I'll gie ye a lift.' And in a moment she was struggling with the almost inert weight of the boy.

With difficulty, he raised both arms a little, and stroked the old woman's grimy face. I saw with amazement that his hands, at least, were still wholly within his command; that it was with deft and tender fingers that he was conveying devotion, love.

'Gran,' he said. 'Gran.'

'I've brocht ye a veesitor, Jamie,' she said. 'A laddie o' the same age as yoursel.' And she turned to me, and in an imploring whisper that would have moved a tougher child than I asked: 'Ye'll bide a wee, young maister? He's that lonesome, my Jamie—and whiles he sees a laddie wi' legs to him gang by.'

'Yes,' I said awkwardly. And I brought myself to come close to Jamie and kneel beside him.

Again with difficulty, Jamie raised his arms, and with the same deft tenderness I had just witnessed he stroked the football boots hanging from my neck.

'Ye play foot-ba?' he asked.

'Yes, I've been playing this afternoon, Jamie.' I was about to add that I was no good at the game, and didn't much care for it. But I realized in time that this would be the wrong thing to say, and fell silent.

'D'ye pick up the ba and rin wi' it?'

'Yes—it's that sort of football.'

'It's an unco queer way wi' a foot-ba.' Jamie laughed softly. 'But ane way or anither, I'd like fine to play foot-ba.'

'Perhaps you will one day, Jamie. When you're better, you will.'

After that, conversation was difficult. But I kept it up for a time, chiefly conscious of shame at the nebulous and mysterious and nasty fears that I had nursed about Jamie's grandmother. Then I felt it was time to go. Had I known beforehand what I was to encounter—I told myself—I would have brought Jamie a present. As it was, I had nothing. Or almost nothing. I felt in the pocket of my shorts, and what my hand came on was a coin. I brought it out. It was a shilling. My intention betrayed itself before I knew its ghastly inadequacy, inappropriateness. What my father called a 'tip' would be utterly wrong. I glanced at the shilling, and suddenly felt a vast relief. On the face of it was not George V, but Queen Victoria. The thing was as good as an antique.

'Jamie,' I said, 'take this. Please take this. It's very old. It would do in a collection. Like a medal.'

Back home, I tumbled it all out. My mother was apprehensive lest I had 'caught' something. But my father was very angry. I supposed he was furious with me for having entered such a house; furious with Jamie's grandmother for having wheedled me into it. But it wasn't at all like that.

'It's appalling!' my father thundered. 'It's a disgrace to the medical and sanitary service of the city.' ('Social services' had not then been thought of.) 'A senile old woman and a helpless child unregarded in such conditions! Paraplegia, as the popular expression has it. Muscular dystrophy, quite plainly. I'll have it out with them! With that damned Town Clerk, or with the Lord Provost himself! Your Jamie and his grandmother will be properly looked after, Donald. That I promise you.'

And so it came about. My father was proud of being an Edinburgh man. *Nisi Dominus frustra*, our civic motto said. Except the Lord keep the City, they labour in vain that build it. The conditions I encountered ought to be held intolerable in any Christian community. My father's indignation and standing were irresistible. Jamie's grandmother was removed to what is now called an Old Folk's Home, and Jamie to some sort of orphanage. I don't suppose that either of them, thus sundered, survived for long.